CURSE OF THE TERRACOTTA WARRIORS

A Maddie Jones Mystery Book 1

MARK DOUGLAS, JR.

*This book is dedicated to my children: Olivia, Owen, and Oliver.
You are my inspiration for Maddie, Jason, and Zac.*

Prologue

Winter 210 B.C.
Capital City of Xianyang, China

THE STRANGE POTION SWIRLED IN the goblet like liquid silver.

I studied the potion before looking up at the alchemist. A young man with hair as dark as his silken robes. A white scar marred his cheek. His face seemed familiar, but I couldn't place him in my memory. He stepped back from the marble pedestal he had set the goblet and knelt to plant his face on the ground.

"My Liege," he bellowed from the floor. "I offer you the drink of immortality—the Elixir of Life!"

I shifted the hem of my golden robe. My hand came free and I grasped the goblet. The silver potion stirred. It moved unnaturally as if in slow motion. I brought the goblet to my nose and sniffed. Nothing. No trace of a smell, but invisible fumes wafted up my nostrils and I suddenly felt dizzy and lightheaded. I saw my image reflected in the mirrored liquid—wrinkles, thinning hair, and a jawline that blended with my neck.

Time had not been kind.

"*Coff—coff*—rise servant—" my voice sounded gravelly from the hacking cough I'd been plagued with for months.

The alchemist climbed to his feet.

I set my elbow onto the armrest of my throne, a magnificent chair of black obsidian inlaid with gemstones and jade. "Where did you come by this?" I asked, admiring the silver drink as I swirled it around inside the cup.

A bead of sweat ran down the alchemist's brow. "Shambhala," his youthful voice bounced off two monumental red pillars and echoed into the throne room's cavernous ceiling. "Beyond the Gobi Desert. High in the mountains amongst the Buddhist monks."

"What did you—*coff, coff*—mix it with?"

"Salt and cinnabar, My Liege. But the secret ingredient was the blood of a pixiu."

"Pixiu blood," I repeated. "So the creature is real?"

The alchemist inclined his head.

My gaze darted to a pair of royal guards standing watch near the entrance. They seemed to take no notice of this revelation, instead staring forward like lifeless marionettes with spears gripped tightly in their hands.

"Did you drink it?"

"I would not dare," the alchemist said. "Yours is the only life worthy of eternity."

I sniffed the potion again. Another bout of dizziness distorted my vision. It must truly be a godly drink to have this effect on me. I started to ask why its fumes caused such lightheadedness when a scratch at the back of my throat made me cough. The physicians said I need not worry, that the cough would subside, but the blood on my handkerchiefs told me otherwise.

Death would come for me soon.

I cleared my throat to smother the cough. I couldn't risk waiting for another alchemist to bring the Elixir. This mysterious drink must be it. So I raised my goblet. "To immortality," I bellowed, and I put the goblet to my lips and drank deeply.

The drink was bitter-cold and thick. It tasted metallic with hints of salt and a strange sweetness I could not place. I swallowed the last drop and slammed the goblet down. My itchy throat no longer tickled. The liquid's healing powers must already be working.

"Now," I rasped, my voice suddenly hissing instead of its usual grumble. "Let's discuss your reward—"

A sharp pain pierced my stomach. Vomit curdled in the back of my mouth "What is this?" I demanded, but no sound escaped my lips. Spittle dribbled onto my chin. I dabbed at the wetness with a silken handkerchief and pulled away fresh droplets of blood mixed with liquid silver. I looked up at the alchemist with wide eyes.

He drew a hidden blade from his robes.

"Guards—" I tried to shout, but instead I retched onto the floor. Dizziness engulfed me. I felt myself falling forward. The world seemed to spin. The next thing I saw was the alchemist standing over me with his dagger pressed to my throat. My insides writhed like an army of soldiers fired a volley of arrows.

"H-help!" I stammered, but my words failed again.

"Qin Shi Huang," the alchemist spoke my name. "Your reign of terror is over. No longer will you slaughter the innocent."

"Who—who—?"

"Who am I?" he asked. "You don't remember?"

I tried to scream for help, but all that came out was a strangled gasp.

The alchemist grabbed a lock of my thinning hair and forced me to look him in the eye. "That's it, take a good look—you know who I am."

I did. That white scar across his cheek. His brown eyes and black hair. He was the spitting image of . . .

"Yes," he breathed. "You killed my father—General Li Fei. You damned his soul when you cursed his men. Now I curse you. The potion you drank will give you eternal nightmares. Your soul will not rest, just like my father's."

The guards were running now. I could see them out the corner of my eye rushing to seize my attacker. But they wouldn't make it in time. The alchemist drew his blade across my neck. Fire lanced across my flesh. My lifeblood poured out from my veins and the room's temperature turned to ice. The last image I saw before darkness swallowed me was the smirk on my assassin's face.

Then the nightmares began . . .

Part One

DADNAPPED

Chapter 1

Present day

THE WORST DAY OF MY life started like this.

I was climbing the rock wall in gym class, hoisting myself up one colorful handhold at a time, when I heard an angry voice yelling at me to speed up.

"One minute to reach the top!" shouted Coach Sinclair, my pudgy PE instructor whose whistle rested on his round pot-belly.

Ever since the first week of school I'd grown to hate the rock wall. It was my worst activity in the whole gym class. Maybe it was because I lacked the upper body strength of boys. Or the sturdy legs of a sprinter. I refused to believe it was because I was a fourteen-year-old girl.

Coach Sinclair blew his whistle. "Time's up, Jones! Get your butt down here."

I blew frizzy-brown hair streaked with purple highlights from my eyes. Then I kicked off the wall with my black Converse shoes and repelled down thirty feet to the basketball court, gasping for air.

Coach Sinclair was there to greet me with a stopwatch in hand and a coffee-stained grin. "Five minutes and twenty-three seconds," he said, showing me the time. "You're slow, Jones. And you can't even reach the top."

"Ah, c'mon, Coach," I groaned. "You know I can't do it. My knees are shaking and I can barely grip the handholds."

"Doesn't matter. The school requires that each student—"

"Pass a fitness test that includes running, climbing, and swimming," I droned in a dull tone. "Yeah, yeah, I've heard your speech already. But you know what? I don't see *you* climbing this thing?"

"*What?!*"

"I mean—" I wracked my brain for what to say next, but before I could think of anything smart, the gym doors burst open. Principal Watson walked in wearing a business skirt and blouse. Two armed police officers joined her. Principal Watson looked around, her eyes settled on me, and she pointed.

"There she is," her voice echoed across the spacious gym floor. "That's Maddie Jones."

The sounds of bouncing basketballs, jumping ropes, and gossiping stopped as students turned to stare at me. The police officers nodded to Principal Watson, then began walking my way.

Oh, no! What was this about? Did they find out it was me who stole the goats and put them in the school's library so they could eat all of the books? Or was it the issue with the front office's aquarium, when the fish went missing and somehow appeared in bathroom toilets all over campus? I promised Principal Watson I had nothing to do with the incident, but apparently she wasn't convinced. What more did she want? The missing fish?

I'd kept one. He was too cute to give back.

The officers' shoes thudded against the court, their handcuffs clinking as they approached.

I had to act fast. I wasn't going to juvie. Not again.

I don't remember running, but the next thing I knew I was sprinting to the girls' locker room where a back exit led to outside tennis courts and the football field. One of the officers shouted, "Hey, Maddie, wait!" and he lunged to catch me.

But I was too fast, and seconds later my tennis shoes were kicking up grass and dirt as I sprinted across the football field. I ran through boys in red and yellow jerseys practicing for next Tuesday's game.

Look, I know I said I'm not much of a sprinter. But when running from trouble you'd be amazed how quickly your legs can move. And you know what's crazy? Running from the police wasn't even why this was the worst day of my life.

Just wait, things are about to get interesting.

Chapter 2

AN HOUR LATER, DONNING GYM clothes soaked in sweat, I ascended the sprawling staircase of the Evansville History Museum, a three-story Colonial building with two wings. As museums go this one was pretty impressive. The place specialized in 16th-century Spanish Exploration of the Americas, which meant loads of Spanish artifacts like swords, coins, and conquistador armor were on display. In some galleries, paintings of famous conquistadors lined the walls. Though, like most museums, there were additional exhibits—like one for astronomy and another for dinosaurs.

Pretty cool stuff.

Now I know you're thinking: Why would Maddie run from the cops and hide out in a museum?

Well, it wasn't to disguise myself as a caveman so I could blend in with the Paleolithic statues. I'd already done that once. Didn't think it would work a second time. Nope, simply put, my dad worked here.

Yep, my dad's big time. He's like Indiana Jones or something. Well, not really, but he does go on digs all over the world to bring back priceless artifacts. He's more of a museum curator, a person who restores historical relics and oversees the management of the museum. And he was the person I came to see. If anyone could get me out of this mess with the police, it was my dad . . . not a lawyer.

Don't even get me started on those guys.

I entered the museum. A fountain burbled in the center of the main lobby. Huge banners hung from a twenty-foot ceiling and showcased the museum's major attractions: black and white photography from Ansel Adams, fossils of a brachiosaurus, and the armor of Spanish conquistador Francisco Vázquez de Coronado.

Neat and all, but I'd seen the stuff a thousand times.

The newest banner was the biggest, and one for an exhibit I'd only seen once—last weekend with my dad and two younger brothers. It depicted a single terracotta warrior from China's *Terracotta Soldiers on the March* traveling exhibit. My dad had recently done something China could not— unlocked a hidden code that helped the Chinese government translate an ancient scroll. They'd sent this traveling exhibit as a way of saying thanks.

If you've never heard of the terracotta warriors of China, don't worry. I hadn't either until they arrived at the museum. They were discovered in the 1970s when Chinese farmers attempted to dig a well. Instead, they unearthed thousands of life-size clay soldiers standing in formation, ready for battle. And when I say thousands, I'm talking about an entire frigging army. They even found horses and chariots. My dad said it was one of the greatest archeological discoveries of modern times.

And because of his efforts, this museum now housed a couple of the statues—two archers, a soldier, and a replica bronze chariot pulled by a team of four horses.

I have to admit they're pretty cool.

"Hey, Maddie," a security guard greeted me behind an imposing front desk. Behind him, TV monitors showed museum galleries where visitors milled about as they enjoyed art and artifacts. It looked like most visitors were in the *Terracotta Soldiers on the March* exhibit. One of the monitors showed me standing in front of Jimmy's desk, a skinny girl of fourteen with bright blue eyes, untidy brown hair tipped in purple highlights, and a studded nose ring.

"Jimmy," I said by way of greeting. "Have you seen my dad?"

"In his office," he said in a bored tone, turning a page of his *Game Informer* magazine.

"Slow day, huh?"

He sighed, not even bothering to look up from the article he was reading. Good thing. If he did, he might've noticed my sweaty gym clothes or spotted the time. School was still in session after all.

I walked past Jimmy's desk and hurriedly entered the stairwell to get out of his view (I didn't want to risk waiting for the elevator). Then I climbed three flights of stairs and reached a door leading into the administration hallway. I grasped its cold, metal handle and twisted—but before I could pull it open a man burst through and crashed into me. His shoulder slammed into my chest, knocking me to the ground. I landed on my butt just as the man dropped something—a metallic silver and green box.

It clanged against the floor beside me. I reached over to pick it up, but the man grabbed it before I could. I noticed a tattoo on the back of his hand as he tucked the device inside his leather jacket. It looked like a Chinese symbol, but it could've been a tribal thing. I wasn't sure.

"Ow," I said, rubbing my leg as I climbed to my feet.

The man glared daggers at me. His eyes were two different colors, one brown, and the other ice blue like a snow husky. Sleek black hair was tucked behind pierced ears.

"Watch where you walk, child," his voice was imbued with an accent I couldn't quite place. Perhaps East-Asia. I started to say something smart, but he turned and bolted down the stairs.

"Hey—no need to apologize or anything!" I shouted after him, but he was in such a hurry I don't think he heard me. "Jackhole."

Dad's office was a quaint room filled with dark oaken furniture, countless books, and miniature statues of conquistadors and Native American art. Dim lamplight illuminated the room in a warm, yellow glow. The place smelled of leather and mothballs. My dad is a tidy guy, and his office is usually impeccable with every book and paper neatly organized.

But today his office looked like an earthquake had hit.

Papers were scattered everywhere. Desk drawers were open, some lying on the floor with their contents spilled across the Persian rug. A bookshelf had been knocked over completely. Dad's computer had been pulled from its base, and as I got closer, I saw its casing had been popped off. Wires and microchips lay scattered beside it. It looked like components were missing, particularly . . .

To be honest, I don't know much about computers, but my brother Jason does. He works on them all the time. He's such a nerd. But just last month I remember he replaced his hard drive—a rectangular device, silver and green in color.

Oh, fetch! The man with the tattooed hand. The metal box. He must've ransacked Dad's office and stolen his hard drive. Which meant . . .

My dad was being robbed!

Chapter 3

I RUSHED DOWNSTAIRS TO THE main lobby. I slammed into Jimmy's desk, short of breath. "Where'd the man with the tattooed hand go?"

"Who?" Jimmy asked as he set aside his *Game Informer* magazine.

"Where's my dad?"

"Is he not in his office?"

"His office has been burglarized!"

"What? Wait—is this another one of your stunts, Maddie?"

"I'm serious!"

Jimmy cringed at my loud voice. "Geez, Maddie, you're gonna scare away the visitors." He smiled at an elderly couple passing by, both of whom glared at me like I was some kind of delinquent. "Look, if it'll make you feel better I'll go up to your dad's office myself. But please quiet down. Your last prank nearly got me fired."

"This isn't a prank, Jimmy."

"You ever hear about the girl who cried wolf?"

"Ugh!" I turned and ran for the exit. Jimmy clearly didn't believe me and I didn't have time to argue. He shouted my name, saying he'd call the cops if something was amiss, but I was already gone.

Outside, I scanned the parking lot for my dad's tan Range Rover. I found it in his usual spot beside the rose bushes. I rushed to the car—and my heart dropped to my stomach. The driver's side door was open, the window busted with glass and blood all over the ground. Inside, the leather seats were slashed as though a knife had cut them. There had been a struggle. A bloody one by the looks of it.

This is more than a burglary, I realized, choking down a sob as I tried to remain calm. Dad was in some kind of danger. But why? Who would want to harm my nerdy father? I whirled around, searching, but I didn't see anybody. Tire marks marred the asphalt right behind the Range Rover. Somebody had peeled out.

They must've forced Dad into the vehicle and drove away.

With my heart pounding and my stomach fluttering like it was filled with dragonflies, I jogged to Eleventh Street and glanced left and right. I didn't see the man with the tattooed hand, and I didn't expect to. I figured he was long gone by now.

Traffic flooded the road. Horns blared from impatient drivers. The sidewalks were full with the throng of businessmen and women, some of whom carried battered briefcases, others talking on cell phones. A few old-timers read the daily newspaper as they walked. Yellow taxis drove by, and it gave me an idea. Perhaps I could find out what was going on at home.

I stepped up to the curb and raised a hand. I'd never hailed a cab before so I didn't know if I was supposed to shout, whistle, or wait. But half a minute later a taxi pulled up and parked. Awesome.

I sat in the back seat. It smelled like a porta-potty. Not awesome. "313 Hazelwood Drive," I said. "And hurry."

The driver, a dark-skinned man wearing a turban hat typical of some Muslim men, turned in his seat and looked me up and down. "How do I know you have money for the fare?"

I glanced down at my gym clothes and realized what the driver must've seen in me. A teenager. No purse or wallet, which meant no money.

But looks can be deceiving.

I took off my shoe, reached into my sock, and pulled out a twenty-dollar bill—my lunch money for the entire week. I shoved it through the tiny Plexiglas window separating us. "Keep the change," I told him.

He grunted and started the taxi meter. I felt the car start moving.

As we joined the traffic, I sat back and tried to settle in for the ride, but my legs were restless and I couldn't stop fidgeting. We couldn't reach my home fast enough. My family lived in a suburb on the outskirts of Evansville. I hated the commute to school every day, but living in a neighborhood was better than living in a condominium.

Outside my window, the city's skyscrapers and downtown area slowly flattened to grasslands and suburbs. White clouds flittered across a blue sky. I didn't have my cell phone or watch on me—I'd put them in my locker right before gym class—and I wondered what time it was. I asked the driver.

"A quarter to three," he told me.

If things had turned out differently today I'd be in sixth period right now. Math class. My least favorite subject. I didn't know what was worse. Running from the cops or using the quadratic formula. I was leaning more toward the quadratic formula when the driver turned down my road. I sat forward and peered ahead . . .

My heart did a somersault. Surrounding my home were dozens of police cars with red and blue lights flashing. Yellow police tape marked off the area. A police officer redirected traffic, and he motioned for us to pull over. I didn't know what to do.

My house was a crime scene!

Chapter 4

THE TAXI DRIVER PARKED, AND I opened the door and bolted. I ducked beneath the yellow police tape and sprinted for my house, a two-story craftsman made of brick and wood with a porch swing out front. Bystanders stood beyond the taped-off area, watching my house as police officers came and went from its front door. I felt sick.

What's happened to my dad? Has he been hurt? Or worse—what if he's been . . .

The thoughts filling my head made my stomach churn. Dad and my two younger brothers were all I had left of my family. I didn't want to imagine life without them. Without *any* of them. I noticed a busted window on the first floor, glass shattered with shards still hanging inside the pane. A forced entry.

The sight made me run faster.

I reached the open front door and rushed inside. Scanning my living room, I saw men in white jumpsuits with fingerprint brushes dusting the area for clues. They dusted the bookshelves, the African artifacts from our vacation overseas, even the photographs of me and the boys. The room's décor would've fit right in with any archeology magazine, the lamps, brown leather sofa, and rugs accented with colorful decorations that looked like they might've come from a World Market store.

All of it was being searched.

Cops in suits and uniforms moved from room to room, latex gloves covering their hands. It made me feel naked. I know, embarrassing. But I dare you not to feel the same when strangers come snooping in your house.

One of the uniformed officers who had a buzz cut of red hair, freckles, and his hat cradled beneath an arm stopped in his tracks to stare at me. "Hey, I recognize you," he said.

I blinked. I certainly didn't recognize him.

"You're Maddie Jones, aren't you?"

I didn't know what to say. My first thought was: Am I on Evansville PD's most wanted list or something? Has one of my pranks gone too far? Is that why the police were conducting an investigation?

No, I told myself. *Something's happened to Dad and you need to find out what.*

"My partner and I came by your school today," the officer said. "You're not in trouble or anything. We just needed to talk."

"Why?" I asked slowly.

"Well, it's your dad, Maddie."

My heart sank. "What's wrong with him?"

The officer dropped his gaze. He wrung the hat in his hands. "Well, Maddie. He, erm—"

"Please," I said, tears blurring my vision despite how hard I was trying not to cry. "Just tell me."

"He's been kidnapped."

Chapter 5

I KNOW THIS MIGHT SOUND dumb, but my brain didn't register what the police officer told me. My dad had been kidnapped? How was that even possible? And who would call it kidnapping if he was an adult?

Maybe the cop should've said dadnapped.

But then it clicked. I finally understood what I'd just been told. My father was missing. I felt my heart beating painfully fast. Was this how heart attacks start? With a tightening chest and the room's temperature heating up? Sweat beaded on my brow. Dizziness blurred my vision—and I stumbled as my vision darkened around the edges.

The freckled police officer caught me. "Easy, it's a lot to take in."

He helped me sit on the sofa. Its leather creaked and felt cold against my legs, bringing me back to my senses. I rubbed my eyes with the palm of my hands, short of breath. I'd never fainted before. Man, it sucked. "Thanks for catching me," I said.

"No problem," the officer said. "You feel okay? Can I get you a glass of water?"

I shook my head.

"Do you run for your school's track team?"

I glanced up and realized the cop was the same officer who tried to catch me in gym class this morning. "Sorry about running away. I thought you guys were going to arrest me."

He smirked. "Why? You have a record?"

I kept quiet. There was no reason to share how much trouble I'd gotten into over the years because of my pranks.

"Gonna plead the Fifth, huh?"

I nodded.

"Smart girl," he said. "All right, stay here. Detective Murphy's in charge and she needs to know we've located you."

He disappeared down the hallway, his boots thudding with purposeful strides, and I found myself sitting on the sofa while a pair of 'snoopers' continued searching my living room for clues. One of the crime scene investigators brushed for fingerprints around my dad's leather recliner. The other inspected objects on the coffee table like Dad's reading glasses and books. Seeing strangers going through Dad's things unsettled my stomach. Seeing his empty chair brought tears to my eyes. Just last night, Dad and I sat in this very room and watched a movie together . . .

I swallowed and glanced away from the investigators. "Can you guys take a break?" I asked in a choked voice. "I could really use a minute alone."

"Sorry, sweetie," the investigator searching Dad's recliner said. "We have to keep working."

"Heartless," I mumbled, but I didn't mean it.

Don't get me wrong—I liked the police. They aren't the bad guys or anything. When you truly need them they're handy and whatnot. But I never liked being told what to do. And I definitely didn't like them searching my home. How many times did I argue with Dad over the years because of my attitude toward authority? He always said I should be respectful and listen to my teachers and blah, blah, blah. Maybe it was time I listened to his advice. Perhaps I should sit here and wait like the police officer told me.

Nah, not today.

I got up and felt a little wobbly in the knees, but otherwise okay. I eased myself to the hallway bracing a hand against the wall. Then I crept toward my dad's study. As I got closer, I heard voices coming from inside his study: a woman's stern voice, and the cop with the freckles.

"You're saying she just showed up at the front door?" the woman asked.

"Yes, ma'am. She has the personality of a wrecking ball. Spunky little girl."

I cringed. Little? I wasn't little.

"I bet," the woman said. "She slipped your grasp, didn't she?"

He grunted.

"All right, let's get her down to the Station. We can reunite her with her brothers and—"

She stopped talking. I had entered the room. My dad's study was a disaster. It looked just like his museum office did—bookshelves knocked over, papers scattered everywhere, and the contents of his desk spilled across the floor. Whoever ransacked the place had been searching for something.

I approached my dad's desk, knelt, and picked up a porcelain elephant statue off the hardwood floor. I'd given it to Dad years ago as a birthday present. I remembered purchasing it from a little girl in India during a family vacation a couple of summers ago. I think the little girl's name was Prisha or Samaira—it didn't matter.

The elephant was broken. I picked up its trunk, body, and separated legs, and placed them neatly on Dad's desk.

"Miss Jones," the woman said, her tone no longer stern. She sounded almost empathetic. "We're doing everything we can to find your father."

"You're Detective Murphy?" I asked.

She nodded, her brown hair pulled back in a severe ponytail. I got the impression Detective Murphy was accustomed to taking charge, despite her small frame. Heck, she was no taller than me—and I'm only fourteen.

"Do you mind if I ask you a few questions?" Detective Murphy asked.

I didn't like answering cop questions. Most of the time my answers got me in even more trouble with the law. But this situation wasn't about me. So I nodded and Detective Murphy fired away.

"When was the last time you had contact with your dad?"

"Breakfast," I said. "We ate oatmeal and talked about the rock wall at school."

"The rock wall?"

"I've been struggling to climb it. Dad gave me words of encouragement and—" I broke away. Tears started building up at the corners of my eyes again.

Detective Murphy's expression softened. She wrote what I'd said into a pocket-sized notebook. "Sorry, Miss Jones. Just a few more questions. Have you noticed anything strange about your dad's behavior lately?"

I shrugged. "He's an archeologist. He loves history and junk. I'd call that pretty strange."

"I'm assuming that's a no, then," she scribbled something into her book. "In the past few days, have you seen anybody snooping around the house?"

I snorted. "Seriously, look at you guys."

"Besides us, Miss Jones."

"No," I said. Then I remembered the man with the tattooed hand from this afternoon. "Wait, there was this one guy. I ran into him at the museum. He vandalized my dad's office and stole his hard drive."

Detective Murphy and the freckled officer shared a knowing look.

"What is it?" I asked.

"We found your dad's home computer disassembled," Detective Murphy said. "The hard drive was missing. I sent what was left with our Criminal Investigation Division to see what they could extract. A security guard from your dad's museum called 911 almost two hours ago. Right now, an investigation team is there searching for clues."

I couldn't understand why anyone would want to destroy Dad's things and steal his hard drives. What could they possibly be looking for? One of his boring history reports?

"Miss Jones, if I sit you down with a sketch artist could you describe the man you saw?"

I nodded. His multicolored eyes still burned vividly in my mind. I wouldn't be able to identify the tattoo on his hand, but I was willing to bet not many people had one like it.

"Good," she said. "We'll head to the Station together in half an hour. Officer Trent," she addressed the freckled cop, "please escort Maddie to her bedroom so she can pack a few belongings."

"Sure thing," Officer Trent said. He motioned for me to join him.

I sighed, not wanting to sleep anywhere else. This was my home. But I knew sleeping here wouldn't be possible tonight. I started to leave so I could go upstairs to my bedroom.

Detective Murphy stopped me. "Oh, and Miss Jones," she flipped a few pages of her book, "One last question. Have you ever heard of a company named Ortega Industries?"

"No. Why?" I asked.

"We have reason to believe Ortega Industries may be behind your dad's disappearance. The company's CEO is a man named—"

But she didn't get to finish.

The house phone suddenly rang, and its shrill tone startled us all.

Chapter 6

DETECTIVE MURPHY YELLED AT everyone in the house to get quiet. The phone kept ringing. She looked at me as though expecting me to answer the call. "It might be the people who kidnapped your father," she said. "Are you willing to talk to them?"

"Why me?" I asked.

"Whoever is on the phone didn't call to speak to the police. They called to talk to whoever lives here."

I didn't want to talk to whoever did this. The person was clearly dangerous. But deep down in my gut, I knew helping Dad was more important to me than getting hurt. So I stepped closer to his desk and reached for the phone.

Detective Murphy grabbed my hand. "Hold on. I'm going to put you on speaker phone. Are you ready?"

The phone rang again.

I nodded.

She hit the speaker phone button.

"Hello?" I said, trying hard to keep the nervousness out of my voice. I was suddenly aware everyone in the house was eavesdropping.

"Oh, thank goodness, Maddie," said a woman's voice, one with a British accent. "The museum called and told me what happened. Have you heard from your father, love?"

All the tension I held in my body before answering the call vanished. It was Tamora Rose, one of my dad's colleagues from work. Like my dad, she was an archaeologist, but she didn't work directly for the museum. Instead, her clients were private collectors. She and Dad had disagreed many times about whether or not historical artifacts should be enjoyed by the public, or hoarded by the wealthy. Even so, the two of them had gone on countless digs together for as long as I could remember.

"No, I haven't heard from him," I said. "Both his office and our home have been vandalized. Tamora—the police are going through Dad's things!"

"Are you hurt, love?"

"No, I'm fine. But . . . I'm a little scared. They're saying Dad's been kidnapped."

Detective Murphy interrupted. "Ma'am, this is Detective Murphy with Evansville PD. I'm concerned about Maddie and her brothers. Do you know how I can contact their mother?"

My eyes darted to a picture hanging on the wall. In the framed photograph, Dad sat beside Mom at a beach restaurant, the sunset behind them casting orange and purples across an ocean view. Mom's auburn hair flowed freely in the wind, and her bright, sea-green eyes matched the water in the background. Her cheeks were warm, and her smile always reminded me of baking cookies.

Dad often told me I looked a lot like her.

"I'm afraid Emily Jones died ten years ago," Tamora said, her voice a bit softer than before. "She had complications with the birth of their youngest child, Zac."

I bit my lip to fight back tears. I was only four when she passed away. I didn't have many memories of her. I mean, come on, how much do you remember from when you were four? But the few memories I did have—her smiles, chocolate chip cookies, kisses goodnight, and the scent of her perfume.

"I'm sorry," said Detective Murphy.

"I often care for the children when their dad travels," Tamora said. "They are more than welcome to stay with me in the city."

Detective Murphy looked at me. "Is this true, Maddie?"

I nodded. Ever since I was a kid in elementary school, I'd stayed at Tamora's place whenever Dad traveled. Sometimes the boys and I would stay for a couple of days, other times a few weeks. The length of time always depended on the progress of Dad's digs. I didn't like staying at her place, but it was a home away from home, in a weird sort of way.

"Can you meet us at the Station, then?" Detective Murphy asked. "To pick up the children and fill out some paperwork?"

"Of course," Tamora said, and she and the detective worked out arrangements.

Meanwhile, I went upstairs with Officer Trent. I packed a backpack of clothes and toiletries. Fed the fish—wink, wink, don't tell Principal Watson. And I made sure to grab a few things for the boys, like their toothbrushes, an extra pair of clothes, and anything else I thought they might need.

Then I headed downstairs and sat on the couch. I waited until Detective Murphy was ready to go. The cops continued their investigation, searching for clues throughout the house, while my mind raced with thoughts of Dad. I hoped he was okay. Since the death of Mom, my biggest fear had always been what would happen to our family if something happened to Dad. Would they put me and my brothers in foster care? Would they split us up? I shuddered at such devastating thoughts. God, where was he? What if he was being tortured? Talk about the worst day ever.

Little did I know, the day wasn't done with me yet.

Chapter 7

THIRTY MINUTES LATER, I FOUND myself sitting in the backseat of Detective Murphy's cop car as she drove along Highway 62 back toward the city. It was now nighttime. Car lights glared through the front windshield from oncoming traffic. The only sounds were the tires roaring on asphalt, and the occasional *thump, thump, thump* from cracks in the road.

"I'm sorry you have to sit in the back like a criminal," the detective apologized. "It's standard police procedure."

"No worries." I didn't really mind. It wasn't my first time sitting in the back of a cop car after all. At least this time my hands were in my lap and not cuffed behind my back. Not that I've committed any serious crimes or anything, but one of my pranks once damaged a McDonald's sign. Let's just say the golden arches aren't supposed to form the shape of a W. "Can I ask you a question?"

"Of course."

"How'd you guys find out my dad was missing?"

Detective Murphy eased the steering wheel left with the curve of the road. "Ortega Industries," she said. "The company manufactures weapons for the U.S. Military. Its CEO is a guy named Rico Raja. Last year, Evansville PD uncovered evidence that Rico planned to sell illegal weapons to an overseas terrorist organization. We've been cooperating with the U.S. government to monitor Rico's movements. He's been under surveillance ever since."

"But what does that have to do with my dad?"

Detective Murphy grabbed a manila envelope from her passenger seat. She passed the envelope back to me.

I opened it, and three photographs fell into my lap. I picked up the top one. The lighting wasn't the greatest, but as we passed street lights interspersed along the road, I was able to make out tiny details. It was a black and white photograph. A bald man was standing with his back to the camera, and he spoke with my dad as they stood on the front steps of the Evansville History Museum. The bald man wore a rich pinstriped suit. He towered over my father by a couple of feet.

"That's Rico," the detective said. "He met with your father Tuesday of last week."

The same day those terracotta warriors arrived at the museum, I thought.

I glanced at the remaining two photographs. The pictures were also taken outside the museum, but I noticed in the top right corner yellow lettering showed the date and times. In both images, Rico's back was to whoever snapped the photo so I couldn't see his face.

"This morning," Detective Murphy said. "I sent a patrol car to pick up your dad for questioning. He didn't answer the door, so the officer circled the home and peered into the windows. When he saw your dad's study the way it was, he called it in. Due to the possible threat Rico poses to our national security, a warrant was issued immediately. I sent additional officers to your school to pick you kids up."

The pieces of today's puzzle were fitting together now.

"Your father has either been kidnapped by Rico Raja," Detective Murphy said. "Or he is working with him."

"My dad wouldn't work with a creep like that."

"That's what I'm here to find out."

"I'm serious," I said. "There was a struggle near his Range Rover. I saw broken glass and blood. He fought whoever took him."

"And I believe you, Maddie. But as a cop, I can't pass judgment until every scrap of evidence is in."

I breathed a quivering sigh. My dad was in more trouble than I thought. "Detective Murphy," I said. "There might be a connection between Rico and an exhibit that arrived at the museum last Tuesday."

"What'd you mean?"

"Well, the museum just got these terracotta warriors—"

Glaring headlights and the loud blare of a horn slammed into the side of Detective Murphy's cruiser. I nearly bit off my tongue from the force of impact. They never tell you how loud car accidents actually are. The crunch and bang of metal is enough to make you go completely deaf. And for a split second, I thought I did.

Then the car flipped end over end, and I had no more time for thoughts.

Chapter 8

I OPENED MY EYES AND discovered I was hanging upside down. My seatbelt cut into my shoulder and neck. It kept me pinned in place. Blood rushed to my head. I felt lightheaded. My ears still rang from the collision with the other vehicle, and my entire body ached.

"Ugh," Detective Murphy gasped. "Oh, my God—"

I glanced around, trying to get my bearings. Broken glass, twisted metal, the constant blare of a car horn—or was that my ringing ears? I wasn't sure. A puddle of water began pooling near my head. I braced my hands overhead and attempted to push my weight up, but I didn't have the strength.

"Oh, my God—" wheezed Detective Murphy.

The vehicle that hit us suddenly pulled away from the wreck. Its tires screeched as it drove in reverse. Then it slammed on the brakes and parked. Through my mangled window, I was able to see that the vehicle was a black van. Its doors opened. Two figures hopped out. From my position upside down on the ground, I could only see their shoes.

Black combat boots.

Fire ignited a puddle of water near the wreck. The strong scent of gasoline filled my nostrils. Oh, fetch! That wasn't water pooling near my head. Flames licked across the asphalt, tracing the spilled gasoline back to its source—the gas tank of Detective Murphy's car.

I didn't want to die. Heck, I certainly didn't want to burn and die. I didn't think Detective Murphy wanted to, either. So I reached up and clawed at my seatbelt buckle. I pushed the button—

—and landed with all my weight on my shoulder. Pain shot into my arm. Gasoline soaked my back. I groaned and rolled onto my stomach. Then I crawled out of the busted window—away from the black van and two approaching figures.

"Maddie—*nghh*—run!" Detective Murphy sounded like she was in a lot of pain.

For a split second, I actually considered running. I mean, seriously, my survival instincts screamed at me to run from the predators and hide. But I knew if I did Detective Murphy would die in her car. I couldn't let that happen to her, so I crawled to her broken window and peeked inside.

Detective Murphy was hanging upside down, strapped in with her seatbelt. The airbag had deployed during the crash, and it might've saved her life . . . but that wasn't the bad part.

A shard of glass the size of a ruler stuck out of her stomach. She gripped it in a bloody hand.

"Oh, my God—" I breathed.

Detective Murphy gritted her teeth. "That's what I've been saying."

I reached inside to unbuckle her strap.

She grabbed my hand. "No—there's no time. You must get out of here. Now!"

Through the passenger side window, I saw the two figures' boots as they approached the wreckage. Flames continued crawling toward the car. Screw it. I might die if I stayed to help the detective, but I couldn't live with myself if I did nothing.

Detective Murphy must've noticed the resolve in my eyes. "You're a stubborn girl, Maddie Jones."

"And you're just now realizing this?" I unclasped her seatbelt.

She fell and cried out in pain.

I reached in and grabbed hold of her vest. Then I pulled with all of my strength to haul her out of the car. She was heavy, but the detective kicked and scrabbled with her feet to try and help. Detective Murphy grimaced with every movement, one hand gripped around the glass shard in her stomach.

We made it to the side of the road. The grass was thick. I laid down beside the detective, hoping the foliage was high enough to keep us hidden. Detective Murphy's breathing became a whimper, but she kept quiet. Strong woman. I admired that. Girl power and whatnot.

The figures walked around the wreckage. They knelt to peer inside the car's busted windows. I noticed they wore tactical assault gear. In their hands were automatic rifles, the kind issued to soldiers by the U.S. government or purchased on the Black Market. I couldn't tell if the figures were men or women, because they wore weird glasses with green dots of light shining from their eyes.

Wait, were those night vision goggles?

Holy cow! These people were armed for World War III. And with those goggles, they'd spot us in no time.

"Where the hell did they go?" the figure on the left said, a man's voice.

The other figure scanned the area. Green lights from the night vision goggles settled on me and Detective Murphy laying in the grass. "Over there!" a female voice said. "They're hiding by the side of the road. Let's grab the girl and get out of here."

"And the cop?"

"Kill her. The boss said no witnesses."

Detective Murphy grabbed her Glock pistol and fired, fired, fired.

Gunshots rang out, and this close to the weapon my ears felt like they might bleed. Bullets struck the female soldier in the chest. The impact knocked her onto her back. But somehow—miraculously—she got right back up. Did she have bulletproof plating or something? It was the only explanation.

The man swore. He raised his automatic rifle and fired in our direction. Bullets whistled overhead and thumped against the grass. I covered my head and screamed. I'd never been under intense gunfire before, and let me tell you it sucked more than anything I'd ever experienced.

Well, the car crash came in a close second.

"Stop—shooting—" the female soldier shouted. "We've been ordered to take the girl alive!"

I realized two things at that moment. One, the bad guys weren't after Detective Murphy, just me. And two, I could save her life if I decided to run. So I did the only sensible thing to do.

I ran.

Detective Murphy's cop car exploded.

The blast catapulted me into the air. The world spun. Blazing heat singed my clothes and hair, and I felt like I would burn alive. I crashed to the ground and landed on my back. My breath left me in a *whoosh*. I worried the gasoline soaking my clothes might threaten to ignite, but a glance told me I was okay.

No Maddie barbeques today. Phew!

Then my vision got fuzzy, and I blacked out.

Chapter 9

MY NIGHTMARE WENT SOMETHING like this.

I was standing in a dark room illuminated by a single torch gripped in my hand. The flickering flame was an ethereal shade of green. It cast ghostly light on cobblestones at my feet, a vaulted ceiling overhead, and a rectangular stone box in the center of the room.

A coffin.

A tomb, I thought. Though I wasn't sure how I knew that. I'd never been inside a tomb before.

Then I heard chains rattling against the cobblestones. I raised my torchlight high, and I saw my dad in iron shackles, chained to the coffin.

"No, get away," my father pleaded, and I realized he wasn't talking to me. He spoke to the coffin. He seemed terrified of whatever was inside of it. He must've been here for days, maybe weeks because his neatly trimmed beard was scraggly, his tweed jacket torn and dirty, and he wasn't even wearing his vintage-framed glasses. He was nearly blind without them.

A bone-rattling hiss cut through the tomb. Behind my dad, just outside the cusp of torchlight, a shadowy figure loomed. I tried to shed light on whoever it was, but no matter how hard I tried my torchlight wouldn't show the figure's details. He, or she, remained cloaked in darkness.

"Open the coffin," whispered the Shadow.

"No, it's not safe." My father cowered from the Shadow, but he also kept his distance from the coffin.

The ground shook. Sand and gravel rained down from the ceiling.

"Release the emperor," the Shadow hissed.

"Never—people will die."

"Enact the curse."

"Get away from me!"

The coffin's lid suddenly flew into the air. It slammed into the vaulted ceiling and came crashing to the ground.

Bony hands emerged. The corpse sat upright. But it wasn't a dead body like I was expecting to see. Instead, it was a clay statue—a terracotta warrior thousands of years old. From head to toe, the warrior was brown, except here and there flakes of paint still clung to its deteriorating face and armor. I'm not sure why, but I felt that beneath its hardened clay exterior a decaying mummy rested within.

The mummy spoke, its voice gravelly like dirt clung to the back of its throat. "Release me, mortal."

My dad screamed.

And I dropped the torch and the light went out.

Chapter 10

I SAT BOLT UPRIGHT, SHIVERING in bed.

There was no tomb. No mummy.

Morning sunlight filtered through my bedside window, tiny dust particles floating in the rays. But this wasn't my bedroom. The sheets were sterile white. A needle was stuck in my arm. A tube stretched from it to an IV bag where some kind of clear fluid dripped. Computers monitored my vitals. A droning *beep*, *beep*, *beep* sounded from the machine. A curtained pavilion separated me from another patient.

Wait, was I in the hospital?

It would explain why the cuts and bruises covering my body were all bandaged up. I didn't remember getting any scrapes. I suppose car crashes and explosions will do that to you. Not good for your health.

The curtain moved, and I thought I saw a shadow flicker across—a humanlike shape. But then there was a knock on the door. A familiar voice called: "Maddie, you awake?" And the shadow behind the curtain disappeared.

It must've been my imagination, the remnants of a shadow from a nightmarish dream.

"Yeah," my voice croaked. I sounded half-dead. "Come in."

My brother Jason entered the room, followed by my youngest sibling Zac. Fair warning about my brothers: they're annoying, they're nerds, but you'll grow to love them.

"Maddie!" Zac rushed to my bedside and gave me a big hug. His embrace hurt my sore body, but I didn't mind. He was my curly-haired bull—a nickname I'd given him because he *bull*dozed his way through sports. At only ten years old, he played soccer, basketball, and football, and he was really good at all of them. I'm not very athletic, so I've always been envious of his ability to walk and chew gum at the same time.

Jason came over and ruffled my hair, his hair blond and spiky.

Ladies—an additional warning. Jason has these boy band looks all the girls go crazy over. It's really annoying, especially when my friends want me to ask him out for them. Don't they know he is only twelve?

Geez!

But don't let him fool you. He's the biggest dork you'll ever meet.

"Guess what, Maddie . . ." Jason adjusted his black-rimmed glasses and smiled ear to ear. A single dimple appeared in his cheek. "While waiting in the hospital lobby, I finally mastered the art of armpit farts."

See what I mean?

I sat up. "What's going on?"

Zac released his hug and sat on a stool. He wore a red jersey and athletic workout pants. "You've been out for nearly a day."

What? I'd been unconscious for how long? Holy cow. That explosion did a number on me.

"And Detective Murphy," I began.

"Don't worry," said Jason. "She's sleeping in the bed over there."

I glanced at the curtained pavilion separating me from the detective. I heard her computer monitor beeping in time to her heartbeat. I sighed in relief.

"She says you saved her life," said Zac.

"Yeah, well, she saved mine too," I said. "What about the soldiers who attacked us?"

Jason and Zac exchanged knowing looks. "They didn't make it," Jason finally said. "They were too close to the car when it exploded."

I didn't know whether to be relieved or not. They may have been assassins, but they were still people. I plopped my head down on my pillow. "Man, yesterday sucked."

"Worst day ever, huh?" asked Zac.

"You have no idea."

There was a rap at the door. "Room service."

A nurse slipped quietly in. She held a tray of food. I smelled oatmeal, bacon, and whiffs of a cinnamon roll. The scents should've made my belly growl. Instead, it unsettled my stomach and made me feel queasy.

The nurse approached my bed. Her hair was storm black and her eyes were painted in dark mascara. She set the tray of food down on a bedside table and smiled. She began to retreat when I saw a strange marking on the back of her hand. I squinted and—oh, my God!

The nurse had the same tattoo as the man who burglarized Dad's office.

Chapter 11

"MADDIE, IS EVERYTHING OKAY?" asked Jason. "You look like you've seen a ghost."

The nurse watched my reaction. I hadn't said anything, but she must've noticed my body tense up. "Erm—" I wracked my brain for something to say. If I showed signs I recognized her tattoo as being the same as Dad's burglar, would she take out a hidden knife and slit my throat? I didn't want to risk it, so I said, "The food looks delicious. Thank you, ma'am."

The nurse smiled and exited the room.

"Oh, I love these babies." Zac grabbed the cinnamon roll from the food tray. He started to take a bite.

I reached over and slapped it out of his hand. It splattered onto the ground.

"Hey—I was going to eat that!"

"*Shhh*—she might be listening."

"Who? The nurse? No way. If anyone's listening it's the cop sitting outside your door."

"There's a cop?"

Jason nodded. "He's security for you and the detective."

"Is he still out there?"

"Probably."

"Will you check?"

Jason walked to the door and peeked outside. "What the heck? Dude's asleep. He was wide awake a minute ago, but now he's got drool hanging from his mouth."

A wave of nausea unsettled my stomach, and this time it wasn't from the smell of food. "I don't think he's sleeping."

"Pretty sure he is." Jason closed the door and rejoined us inside. "He's snoring like a grizzly bear."

I shook my head. "What if he was drugged?"

Zac picked up a strip of bacon and sniffed it. "Who would drug a cop?"

"The nurse," I said. "I think she's trying to kill me."

"Okay—you're officially whacko," said Jason. "The cop's just snoozing."

I didn't think so. The nurse's tattoo was too similar to the man who burglarized Dad's office. I was willing to bet she was in league with him. Plus there were the soldiers who caused the car crash. Who sent them? And why did they want me captured alive? A scary thought struck me. What if the bad guys also came after Jason and Zac?

We were sitting ducks inside this hospital room. Heck, the nurse was probably in the hall right now, waiting to come back inside once I'd eaten the food. We needed to get out of here. But I couldn't simply walk out the front door. She'd spot us, which meant we needed a Plan B—another means of escape.

I swung my feet over the edge of the bed and ripped the IV out of my arm. "Ow," I hissed at the sting. Blood trickled from the wound. I wiped it away with the sleeve of my gown.

"Whoa, Maddie, what are you doing?" Jason tried ushering me back to bed.

I shooed him away. "I need clothes."

"What you *need* is to lay back down."

I stood up. Everything swayed. The room felt like it was a ship being tossed by waves. My hands trembled. As a kid, I'd always assumed I was invincible. Note to self: you're not Super Girl, Maddie Jones.

Zac leaned over the tray of food. "So what's wrong with the grub? Smells yummy to me."

"It might be poisoned," I said.

"Poisoned?" the boys said together.

"Dang, keep your voices down." I rubbed my eyes to clear my blurry vision, then I explained how I'd found Dad's office destroyed and bumped into a man fleeing the scene with a tattoo on his hand.

"Hey, the nurse had a tattoo on her hand," said Zac.

"Hold up," said Jason. "Are you saying these people with tattooed hands know where Dad is?"

"I think so," I said. "They might be assassins. Or maybe just thieves. I really don't know."

"Well, if they know where Dad is . . ." Jason crossed his arms. "Then we gotta find out who they are and confront them."

"Confront them? They could be super dangerous."

Zac stood from his stool with a clenched fist. He looked ready to fight. "Who cares? We need to find Dad!"

God, I loved my brothers. It didn't matter that I'd nearly been killed by soldiers on the road. Or that a secret society of tattooed hands might be out to get us. They would do anything to save our father. I hoped I could muster the same courage.

Jason knelt and unzipped his backpack. He reached inside and pulled out a pair of clothes. "Tamora drove us by the house to gather a few things," he explained as he handed them over.

"Tamora?" I asked.

"We stayed at her place last night. She dropped us off at the hospital on her way to work. So do you have a plan?"

Not really, I thought.

The first thing I needed was to get out of this gown. I couldn't go running from the hospital looking like a mental patient on the loose. Plus the thing barely covered my body. Don't even get me started on how little it covered my backside. Let's just say a chill breeze tickled my hiney.

The boys turned around and I began changing. "With the front door blocked there's only one way out . . ." I pulled off the gown and slipped into blue jeans with rips in the knees and donned a black tank top with a punk rock band's logo—a mohawk-haired octopus playing the drums. Then I threw on my favorite dark denim jacket, which I loved because of its many pockets and zippers and the stylishly built-in hoodie. "And it's through that window."

Jason and Zac looked at the window, and they gave me two different reactions. Zac's face lit up in a thrilled smile, apparently seeing the window as an opportunity to try those parkour moves he'd been watching on YouTube lately. But Jason's face turned green and he looked like he might hurl.

"Do you realize we're five stories high?" Jason asked.

I laced up my black Converse high tops. "No, but I don't see another way out of this room. Do you?"

Jason looked around. He groaned.

I moved to the window and peered outside. Morning sunlight streamed through gaps of downtown skyscrapers, illuminating a quiet street fifty feet below with cars parked on both sides. A fire escape with a set of spiraling stairs was located to my left. The window latch was loose. I clicked it to OPEN, and the window swung out with an easy nudge. A cool breeze fluttered in. It billowed the curtains, including the one separating the beds. I heard Detective Murphy stir.

"Maddie, is that you?"

Sorry, Detective, I thought, hopping onto the window seal so I could ease out onto the ledge. *But if you stick with me you're going to get killed.*

After all, she had only just met me and already she was in the hospital. And if I stayed with her, I'd likely never find out what was going on with Dad. I only hoped in the next twenty-four hours I wouldn't be dead.

Chapter 12

HAVE YOU EVER REGRETTED your choices immediately after you made them? I know I have. Sure, I like to act as though I have my stuff together, but sometimes I make the dumbest choices.

Like right now. Holy cow, what was I thinking?

"Escape through the window," I chided myself, sidestepping closer to the fire escape with my back pressed firmly against the brick wall. Wind billowed my clothes. A treacherous fall loomed five stories beneath me. My Converse high-tops hung halfway over the ledge. "Yeah, this was a stupid decision."

Jason edged along the wall beside me. He mumbled cuss words beneath his breath. I had no idea he knew such words. Zac followed after him, grinning ear to ear like we rode an epic thrill ride and he was having the time of his life.

I glanced toward the fire escape. It was twenty feet away. "We're almost there!" I shouted.

"Shut up!" said Jason, his breathing quick and heavy. "Or you'll make me fall."

I stopped talking. The last thing I needed was Jason falling to his death. I could live with myself if I fell, but if one of my brothers . . .

Wait, if I fell, I would die. Blah, I think you get my point.

I reached the fire escape. I grabbed its metal railing and hopped over. The platform clanged and shook when my shoes stomped down. The platform felt rickety and old. Red dust coated my hands from touching the rusting metal. I blew hair from my eyes and glanced toward my brothers. Jason was five feet away and moving slowly. Sweat beaded on his brow despite the cool autumn air. I held my breath as he reached for the fire escape railing with trembling hands. He squeezed the railing in a white-knuckled grip.

"H-help me," his voice quivered.

I reached out and helped him climb over the railing and onto the platform. He stumbled to his knees and kissed the metal flooring.

I rolled my eyes. "Wow, you're really brave. And you plan on confronting assassins?"

"Shut up," he said. "I can't stand heights."

Zac stopped edging closer. Instead, he stood several feet away staring at the empty air between him on the ledge and me on the fire escape.

"Oh, no you don't," I said, realizing what must be going through his mind.

"What?"

"You're thinking of jumping onto the railing, aren't you? Just like those people in the YouTube videos doing parkour."

"No, I'm not."

"Yes, you are. I can see it in your eyes."

Zac smirked. "Okay—I am—but I can make it, Maddie. It's not that far."

"No, Zac."

He licked his lips and rocked forward onto his toes.

"I said, NO!"

He jumped. My heart stopped beating for a fraction of a second. Zac hurtled weightlessly forward, flailing his arms with open hands so he could grab onto the fire escape railing. Nothing but air and death loomed beneath his feet. I slammed into the railing to catch him if he fell—

—Zac landed on the fire escape and gripped the railing tight.

"See, I told you I could make it," he panted.

The rusty handrail snapped. Zac fell backward, shouting as he plummeted toward the street. I reached out to grab his shirt—but I missed. He slipped beneath my hands.

"ZAC!" I screamed.

Jason dove from his knees and caught him by the wrist through slits in the metal railing.

"Agghh!" Zac cried in pain as his body swung forward and struck the platform. His feet kicked uselessly. He dangled from the fire escape. "Nggh—don't let go!"

"I won't," Jason promised through gritted teeth. The veins in his arms bulged from the strain of holding Zac's weight.

I knelt and grabbed Zac by the back of his shirt. Together, Jason and I pulled him up. Zac climbed onto the fire escape. We hauled him over the railing, then we sprawled onto our backs, sweating and breathing deeply. When I finally managed to catch my breath, I climbed to my feet.

"You scream like a girl, Zac," I said.

He stood and rubbed his wrist where Jason had caught him. "No, I don't."

"Well, no more parkour for you. You suck at it."

Jason's knees wobbled as he stood up. "Do you think anybody heard all of that?"

I glanced down at the street to see if anyone was lurking. It appeared empty save all of the parked cars. "I don't think so," I said. "But that doesn't mean someone hasn't spotted us from an apartment window. C'mon, let's get out of here."

We descended the spiraling staircase to the street. Gentle sunlight filtered through trees interspersed every few feet along the sidewalk. A lady walking her dog approached, but she was so glued to her phone she didn't take much notice of us. The stretch of road was fairly quiet—and good thing, too, considering all the commotion we had just caused. A street sign read LINCOLN AVENUE.

We're only a few blocks from the museum, I realized. I turned on my heel and marched up the street.

"Where are you going?" Jason demanded.

"Back to the scene of the crime," I said. "If we're going to find clues revealing what happened to Dad, then his office is the best place to start."

Chapter 13

THEY SAY CROOKS WILL REPORT back to the scene of the crime during a police investigation. Each criminal is different, their motivations for returning ranging from sick pleasure to seeing the art of their handy work. Sometimes they return to make sure the crime scene is clean. Meaning, they didn't leave evidence behind. And how would I know? Well, I enjoy watching cop shows with my dad on Thursday nights.

What? Did you think I knew because I'd done it? No way!

Yes, I have a juvie record—but I'm not a dangerous criminal or anything. I just like silly pranks. It's not my fault those pranks sometimes get me in trouble with the law. Besides, I'd never be dumb enough to return to a crime scene if I knew I might get caught.

Well, until today.

Technically, the crime scene my brothers and I came to investigate wasn't one of mine. Thank goodness. But it was a place I was as familiar with as my bedroom.

My dad's museum office.

"The museum doesn't open for another hour," said Jason, wriggling the back door's handle. We were on the loading dock where new shipments of artifacts often arrived, but the glass door wouldn't budge. It was locked. "So how the heck do we get inside?"

"How should I know?" I mumbled between bites of delicious cinnamon-raisin bagel. I hadn't eaten since yesterday, and as we walked the distance here we passed a pastry stand. Sometimes people are looking out for you, and I strongly believed the bagel vendor had been placed there by the hand of God to deliver me this sweetly-flavored bread.

"Check beneath the mat," prompted Zac.

Jason groaned. "This isn't our house, Zac. The museum wouldn't leave a key to priceless artifacts in such an insecure place."

"Just check."

Jason obliged him and lifted the mat. "See—no key— are you happy?"

I finished my last bite and chased it down with the last of my orange juice. I tossed the empty bottle into a trash bin near a little garden bordered by loose stone tiles. Just like the front of the museum, the loading docks were richly decorated with flowers and statues. The museum liked to keep up with appearances, after all.

"We're running out of time." Jason cupped his hands on the glass door and peered inside. "I thought you had a plan, Maddie."

I started whistling a Joan Jett song: *Bad Reputation.* I loved songs about rebellious women. Plus, I was feeling much better after finishing my breakfast. I strolled over to the garden and picked up a stone tile, humming song lyrics: *I don't give a damn about my bad reputation.*

"Erm, Jason," said Zac.

"What?" Jason continued gazing into the museum.

"You might want to move."

"Why?" He turned around.

I threw the stone and it smashed into the glass door. The sound of breaking glass rang out. It was really frigging loud.

"Geez! What the heck is wrong with you?" Jason shouted.

"Look, Dad's missing." I stepped across the threshold. Shattered glass crunched beneath my feet. "And every second he's gone is another chance he could potentially die. If we're gonna find him, we can't let obstacles like locked doors stop us."

"Yeah, but you set off the alarm."

I strained my ears to listen. Sure enough, a droning *wee-woo-wee-woo* echoed throughout the museum.

I shrugged. "Nothing we can do about it now. If we're lucky, we'll have twenty minutes to investigate Dad's office."

"And if we're unlucky?" asked Zac.

"Then we'll have ten minutes. Better run."

Chapter 14

WE WERE OUT OF BREATH by the time we reached Dad's office. On our way here, we raced past the terracotta warriors' exhibit. I recalled Detective Murphy's photographs of Dad meeting with the CEO of Ortega Industries. Rico Raja approached my dad on the same day the exhibit arrived. What interest did he have in the ancient warriors? What was he after? And why would he kidnap Dad?

"It took us three minutes to get here," said Jason, pulling his iPhone from his pocket and inputting a passcode. "I'm setting a timer for five minutes. When it goes off—that's it—we need to leave whether we've found anything or not."

I walked past him to enter Dad's office.

He grabbed my arm. "Five minutes, Maddie. I'm serious."

I shrugged his hand away. "I heard you the first time. Don't be so uptight."

His eyebrows arched in surprise. "Felony. Breaking and entering. That's all I'm going to say."

The alarm continued blaring. I figured we needed to be out of here in three minutes, just to be safe, but I didn't bother telling him that. Jason was wound so tight, I figured his head might explode if he knew how quickly the cops might arrive. Perhaps he wasn't used to breaking rules like I was.

"Whoa, look at this place." Zac ducked beneath the yellow police tape marking Dad's office as a crime scene. "Whoever did this wasn't messing around."

I stepped in behind him. Dad's office was still a disaster. Papers, books, and desk drawers remained scattered across the floor. Artwork and Native American statues were knocked over as well. The only thing missing was his computer. I guess Evansville PD had confiscated it as evidence.

"What are we looking for?" asked Zac.

"I'm not sure," I said.

Jason groaned.

"Look," I stomped my foot in frustration. "The only thing I know is that a business tycoon kidnapped Dad—and all because he knows something about the terracotta warriors. So, I don't know, search for anything related to those things."

Jason didn't argue. He knelt beside the bookcase lying on the ground, picked up a book, and rifled through its pages. Zac lifted a corner of the Persian rug and felt around for loose floorboards.

Meanwhile, I went to Dad's desk. Dozens of important-looking memos and research papers were strewn across it. Scanning their titles didn't tell me anything useful. I rummaged through the few desk drawers not shoved onto the floor. Inside one of them, I found a mini-compass attached to a thin black cord.

I knew it, I thought.

This compass was further proof Dad wasn't working with Rico. He never traveled without this compass necklace. He considered it a good luck charm, but the compass symbolized so much more.

Mom gave it to him the year I was born.

"If you ever lose your way," Dad told me she would say. "Then this compass will guide you home."

I put the compass necklace on and resumed searching.

A miniature statue of an Apache Indian firing a bow caught my attention. It rested beside a framed photograph of Mom when she was pregnant with Zac. The picture was taken one month before she died, and I knew Dad cherished it deeply. Another picture, taken years after she passed, showed the three of us kids clinging to Dad—all smiles. But that one had fallen over, and its glass was cracked.

I picked up the frame and brushed off the glass.

The photo fell out.

A yellow parchment was taped to the back of the picture—and cash, but it wasn't American money. It looked like Chinese currency. "Hey, I think I found something."

"What?" the boys stopped what they were doing and rushed to my side.

I pulled the tape off the parchment and showed them the folded document along with the money.

"Is that Chinese money?" asked Zac.

"I think so."

"Chinese currency is called renminbi," said Jason. "Or yuan."

"Do you enjoy knowing useless facts," I said. "Or is nerding out just your thing?"

"Shut up." He snatched the folded parchment out of my hand.

"Hey," I protested.

But he unfolded the paper, and what we saw made me forget about scolding him. It looked like a map, complete with markings and Chinese lettering. Along one side, a drawing depicted a single terracotta warrior. Beside it, writing—in Dad's angled script. "Beware," it read.

And that's all we got to read.

Because men shouting sounded from the direction of the main lobby, followed by the distinct static of police radios.

Crap.

We'd run out of time!

Chapter 15

WE RUSHED FROM DAD'S third-floor office and darted to the stairwell at the end of the hall, only to discover a pair of cops making their way up.

"Crap," whispered Jason. "We're trapped."

"No, the other stairwell," I said.

We bolted down the hallway at an all-out sprint. The cops emerged as we turned the corner, talking, but I don't think they spotted us because I heard them discussing dinner plans and a Mexican restaurant located downtown. Their voices faded as we ran. I didn't hear any boots stomping down the hall after us.

Phew! That was close. But we weren't in the clear yet, because I was pretty sure more cops searched the museum. Luckily, we didn't find anyone patrolling the second stairwell, so we crept downstairs. When we reached the ground level, I creaked open the stairwell door just enough to peer outside.

A third cop approached.

He was lean and his uniform looked baggy like it was a size too large. He searched museum exhibits, his flashlight shining on wax statues of cavemen making fire. He swept his light, and Paleolithic women gathering berries in woven baskets gleamed into view. He slowly made his way to our position.

"See, I told you we're trapped," said Jason.

I eased the door closed. "Maybe not."

One year ago, I found myself in a similar situation. I had spray-painted mustaches on billboards all over town, the cops were on to me, and I ran inside the museum to hide. On that particular day, I had just enough time to disguise myself as a cavewoman and pretend to pick berries, frozen in place. I got away.

But now, we didn't have the same advantage. The Paleolithic clothing was in another section of the building. But I had a different idea. All it required was blending in with museum artifacts as we made our escape. If the cop would just keep up his patrol of museum artifacts . . .

I cracked the door back open and peeked into the museum.

The cop turned a corner and strolled down a hall leading to exhibits of Spanish conquistadors.

"Yes," I breathed. "Follow me."

I opened the door wider and slipped out of the stairwell. I trailed silently after the cop. If I were him, I wouldn't bother retracing my steps if I felt I'd searched the museum thoroughly enough. So we followed him, darting from shadow to shadow, hiding behind statues and display cases and anything else we could find.

A few minutes later, Zac bumped a display case and its glass covering rattled. The cop stopped his patrol and swept his light in our direction. I leapt behind the armor of a conquistador and stood tall like I hid behind a tree. Jason ducked behind a trash bin. Zac froze behind the display case he had bumped—gold and silver Spanish doubloons resting inside. After shining his light on the armor and doubloons, the cop cleared his throat and continued his patrol.

Zac silently mouthed: "Sorry."

We resumed trailing the cop. When we finally reached the back of the museum near the loading dock with the busted glass door, I knew we were in trouble. It was busy with the hustle of police and the bustle of museum employees.

The cop we'd been following joined the group. "All clear," he said.

"Nothing, huh?" said a second officer with bushy eyebrows and a stocky build. "Perhaps a couple of kids smashed the window."

"Maybe," said the cop we'd been following.

As they spoke, I crouched beside a wall overlooking our exit. The shadows here were dark enough to stay hidden. The boys crept up beside me. I counted two cops and six employees—all people I recognized because they worked with my dad.

"Looks like we need to see security footage," said the stocky officer. "Which one of you is Jimmy Trout, head of security?"

"I am," a barrel-chested man replied. He stepped clear of the museum employees mingled together and stuck out a hand.

The stocky officer shook it. "Do you have access to the security cameras?"

"Certainly," said Jimmy. "Right this way." He led the officer toward the main lobby, away from our position. But the cop we had trailed stayed behind. Dang. Why couldn't both of them have gone?

Jason nudged me. "They're going to see video of you busting that window."

"Who cares?" I said. "We'll be gone by the time they figure it out."

"How? They're blocking the exit."

Sure enough, the remaining police officer blocked our path as he began asking the employees questions. He recorded their responses in a pocket-sized notebook. Stupid detective wannabe. Why couldn't he stop being an overachiever and let everybody go?

"I arrived a few minutes ago, sir," said a grandmotherly woman when asked a question. It was Franny, the elderly lady who worked in the gift shop. Seeing her suddenly gave me an idea.

"Okay, I have a plan . . ." I faced the boys and gave them instructions.

"That won't work," Jason groaned.

"Well, do you have a better idea?"

"No."

"That's what I thought." I stood and straightened my clothes. "So follow my lead and put some confidence in your voices."

The three of us stepped out from our hidden position and walked purposefully toward the group. The officer saw us approaching. We must've startled him because he squared up and rested a hand near his gun. Calmly, and with as much cheer as I could muster, I directed my focus to the grandmotherly woman—who loved to bring us chocolate chip cookies almost weekly.

"Hi, Franny!" I said.

Franny's face lit up when she saw us. "Maddie? Goodness gracious, child. Shouldn't you be at school?"

The cop relaxed his threatening posture, but only slightly.

I inhaled deeply, then began my lie: "Dad left unexpectedly to assist the Chinese government on a dig, but he's such a klutz. You know how he gets, so forgetful. He brought everything but the kitchen sink—the sink being his notes on the terracotta warriors. Have you seen the new exhibit China sent to our museum? Super impressive."

"Wait . . ." the cop said slowly. "Do you know these kids?"

"Oh, yes," Franny answered. "They are Dr. Hank Jones' children."

"He left us a key to the museum," I went on. "Tamora Rose—my dad's colleague—you do know Tamora, right, Franny?"

"Lovely woman," she nodded.

"Well, she's out in the car waiting. We rushed to retrieve Dad's notes before school, but we heard a crash of some kind and it startled us. We hid until we thought it safe to come out."

"Hold up." The cop thumbed through pages of his notebook. "I thought your dad went missing."

"Indeed, he did," Jason piped up. "All the way to China. But he hasn't been kidnapped if that's what you're thinking. He's had this trip planned for months."

Bless my brother. Why couldn't he act so confident and brave all the time?

"And if you don't mind, officer," I said. "We need to get these notes to him. The Chinese government is depending on his expertise."

The cop narrowed his eyes. "There's just one problem," he said. "I don't see any notes in your hands."

"Ah," Jason reached into his pocket and pulled out the yellow parchment we'd found. "Wanna see them?"

The officer narrowed his eyes. He snatched the paper out of Jason's hand and unfolded it.

Zac finally spoke: "Can you read Chinese, officer?" His voice sounded innocent. Ooh, he was good. My little protégé in training.

The cop cleared his throat. "All right, the three of you get to school." He stepped aside so we could exit.

Oh, yeah! Maddie the genius strikes again. I smiled at Franny and told her to save me a batch of her delicious chocolate chip cookies, then my brothers and I walked out of the museum. The cop handed Jason the parchment as we exited. Five minutes later, we strolled down Riverside Drive with the sun gleaming brightly, free as songbirds, feeling like we had just completed the perfect crime.

Chapter 16

WE NEEDED A PLACE TO lie low, somewhere with a quiet table, enough lighting to study a map, and lunch. Most importantly lunch. Turoni's Pizzeria & Brewery sounded yummy, and I remembered they had deep booths where we could discuss the map without fear of eavesdroppers. The restaurant was only a few blocks from the museum, so the boys and I walked the busy sidewalks toward the restaurant. Pedestrians jostled by us, some hailing cabs, talking on their phones, or grabbing a bite to eat from one of the many vendors at each corner.

For the most part, we walked in silence.

Jason finally broke it. "Who is the business tycoon?"

"What?" I glanced over my shoulder. Paranoia told me we were being followed, but I didn't see anyone suspicious.

"You said something about a business tycoon kidnapping Dad."

"Oh, that," I said. "His name is Rico Raja. He's the CEO of a weapons manufacturing company."

"What company?"

"Ortega Industries. Why?"

Jason's cell phone appeared in his hand. He started typing with his thumbs as we walked. "I want to do some research."

"Why would a business tycoon kidnap Dad?" asked Zac. His shorter legs struggled to keep up with our longer strides.

"I dunno, Zac," I said. "The guy makes weapons. Dad is an archaeologist. It's a strange pairing."

Jason grunted.

"Find something?"

"Yeah," he said. "Quite a few news articles about Rico and Ortega Industries. His company is responsible for making ballistic missiles, heavy-duty assault rifles, and Kevlar bullet-proof armor."

A memory of Detective Murphy shooting the soldier in night-vision goggles flashed before my eyes. Bullets knocked her over, but she got right back up. Mystery solved. The soldiers wore Kevlar.

"And you'll find this interesting. Rico was recently interviewed by *Archeology Magazine*."

I arched an eyebrow. "That is interesting. What's it say?"

"Here, take a look—" Jason handed me his phone. The article was topped with a picture of Rico donning an expensive-looking suit while he stood amidst a large collection of historical artifacts, paintings, and relics.

FORTUNE 500 BUSINESSMAN
HAS A PASSION FOR HISTORY

by Sophia Valentino

Rico Raja, the CEO of weapons development company Ortega Industries, has been an avid collector of antiquity since early childhood, *writes Sophia Valentino, Special Correspondent.* In September of this year, I had the privilege of touring his private collection at Ortega Headquarters, a high-rise office building located in the heart of downtown New York City. As I admired historical relics ranging from Leonardo da Vinci paintings to jewel-encrusted crowns from India, Rico led me to a display case to gloat over his most prized possession—a small, unremarkable Rosary dating back to ancient Rome.

"I discovered the Rosary in a garden when I was six years old," says Rico, removing the glass case so I could hold the artifact in my hand. "From that moment, I was enraptured by history and wanted to know more about our past."

An alarmingly large and powerful-looking man, Rico has since been using his substantial resources to scour the world for historical artifacts. "Throughout my travels," says Rico. "I have conquered countless tombs and unearthed relics thought to be myth, but I have never had full access to China's archaeological sites."

China, a notoriously private country, has been weary of foreign archaeologists in the years following Colonial British efforts to unearth Egypt. "I aim to change all that," says Rico. "I hope to convince the country's leaders that opening the Tomb of the First Qin Emperor will be good for China's economy."

I stopped reading. "This was written one month ago."

"So that's what he's after," said Zac. "Rico wants another artifact for his collection, and he needs Dad's help to get it."

Something didn't sit right with me. "Maybe," I said. "I mean, did you hear how he spoke? He sure liked the word *conquer*. Rico sounds like someone who is used to getting what he wants."

"He's worth several hundred million," Jason informed.

"Exactly. Typical rich man syndrome. And guys like that *take* if they can't have." I thought for a moment. All those artifacts in his collection. What would one more add, really? A new trophy? Boring. Rico struck me as the kind of man who enjoyed the thrill of a chase. "He has artifacts," I said. "Maybe he wants something *more*."

"Yeah, but what?" asked Zac.

"I'm not sure." I handed Jason back his phone. "What can you find on the First Qin Emperor of China?"

"Just a sec—" Jason went back to searching online. Meanwhile, we turned down North Main Street. Turoni's restaurant sign loomed a block ahead, and my mouth salivated at the prospect of pepperoni pizza and ice-cold Coca-Cola.

"Okay, got it," said Jason. "The First Qin Emperor of China commissioned the construction of an army of terracotta warriors to keep guard over his tomb. His reign was brutal—"

A man suddenly stepped out of a dark alleyway, blocking our path. He towered over us, wearing a black V-necked shirt, blue jeans, and a camo jacket. His eye twitched, and the white scar across his cheek stretched grotesquely.

"Don't even think about running," he growled, and he pulled his jacket open just enough so we could see the butt of a holstered pistol.

Chapter 17

WHAT'S THE FIRST THING YOU do when you're told not to do something? Most of the time you do it. I'm no different, especially when someone in authority gives the command. But in this case, I decided to do one thing extra before disobeying the goon's order.

I kicked him in the soft spot, making him sing soprano.

"Run!" Jason shouted, and the three of us raced into the pizza restaurant.

The place smelled amazing. A sweet aroma of baking pizzas mixed with something else I couldn't quite put my finger on. Apple cinnamon? Oh, maybe they were making those dessert pizzas. Ah, man, why'd that goon have to be so rude? We could be enjoying slices of cheesy pizza and looking over Dad's map.

Instead, we dashed past startled patrons and servers. I heard the hostess yell something about waiting to be seated, but her words cut out as we slammed into swinging doors labeled KITCHEN.

I crashed into a chef wearing a white apron and hat. He was in the middle of throwing pizza dough into the air. It landed on the ground, and he shouted cuss words I dare not repeat.

An exit in the back caught my attention. The boys must've seen it, too, because they ran on ahead. I jumped the dough, then ran past a cook sprinkling pizza toppings and another pulling bread out of an oven. Dang it, you've got to be kidding me.

It was mozzarella cheesy bread.

I got a whiff of it as I darted by, and temptation got the best of me. I snatched it up and kept on running.

Holy cow, the bread was hot!

Blowing on it didn't help, so I tossed the cheesy bread from hand to hand as I ran for the exit. I reached the door and bolted outside. Right before the door swung closed, I caught a glimpse of the goon with the scarred face charging into the kitchen. He was chasing us. Maybe I should've kicked him harder.

"He's on our tail!" I shouted at the boys, and I saw them rushing to a chain-link fence at the far end of the back alleyway. They jumped onto the fence, climbed to the top, and swung over to the other side.

The goon burst out of Turoni's kitchen. He looked left and right, and found me. I realized I wouldn't be able to jump the fence in time. A cracked door next to the fence led into an old apartment building.

"Get to Tamora's place!" I yelled.

"We're not leaving you!" shouted Zac. He started climbing back over the fence.

"Go, Zac! I'll meet you guys there!" I ran into the apartment building. A stairwell led up.

Eating and climbing stairs is not easy to do, but I managed to get a bite of delicious cheesy bread. God, it tasted like heaven. But I nearly choked from the exertion of running, so I dropped the bread. What a waste.

Below, I heard the goon stomping up. His breathing sounded like an enraged bull. It unnerved me. He was close. I exited the stairwell on the second floor. A long hallway stretched before me. No exits in sight. I slammed the hallway door shut, then ran straight ahead.

The goon crashed through the door. He busted its hinges like Juggernaut from those X-men comics. Whoa, this guy was scary.

A resident exited her home. She started to close the door, but I bumped into her and ran into her apartment. She yelled at me in Spanish, and I didn't need to know the language to understand she wasn't happy.

A bare-chested man sat on a red-flannel couch in nothing but whitey-tighties. Gross. He played Xbox and ate Cheetos. Super gross. A headset was on his head, and a Battle Royale game was onscreen. Kind of cool.

"Hi, there," I said as I jumped the coffee table.

"What the—" he sat forward so quickly his bowl of Cheetos went flying.

A sliding glass door led out onto a balcony. I shoved it open. Outside, I had two choices: jump one story down and potentially snap an ankle. Or swing over to the adjacent balcony.

Inside the apartment, the Juggernaut goon ran straight through the coffee table. Magazines, drink coasters, and a bowl of potpourri exploded into the air.

I had to make my decision. Now.

I swung over to the next balcony. Good choice, because its sliding door was already opened. Lucky me. I ran inside—and I stumbled into a tripod holding a painting canvas. A woman screamed, brush in hand, and paints splashed everywhere. I was tagged pretty good—reds, whites, greens, and blues splattering my face and clothes. Paint got on my favorite dark denim jacket. You've got to be kidding me!

"Sorry," I said.

The woman shouted for her husband.

I groaned. What happened to my luck? I glanced toward the balcony, but I didn't see the goon yet. Maybe he only had one speed—forward. Given his massive size, parkour probably wasn't his thing. Great for me, because I could use the extra time to put some distance between us. I darted out of the apartment and into the hallway—

The goon tackled me.

We crashed to the ground in a tangle of arms and legs. The impact hurt. I mean, seriously, a grown man the size of a grizzly bear just slammed into me—a fourteen-year-old girl.

He stank of sweat. I struggled to break free. A strong hand grabbed my wrist, and I think he was attempting to wrap me in a hold so I couldn't fight back. Not happening, dude.

I poked him in the eye.

Yep, I pulled a Three Stooges and gave him a good jab. He cried out in pain, clutching his face. I broke free and climbed to my feet. He lashed out, but with his wounded eye, he missed. I ran down the hall. And the last I saw of him, he flailed in pain as I rushed to get away.

Chapter 18

TWENTY MINUTES LATER I REACHED the Plaza Condominiums, a thirty-story skyscraper of luxurious living overlooking the city and Ohio River. As condos go, this one was pretty posh. You name it and the place had it. Doorman to carry your luggage? Check. Mercedes parked on every curb? Double check. The snootiest people you will ever meet? Don't even get me started.

Did I mention this was Tamora's home?

Yep, I hated the place.

Not that Tamora was a mean person or anything. It's just that . . . well . . . ever since Mom died I feel like Tamora has tried to fill a void she can't possibly fill. Maybe you can only understand if you've lost a parent. Or if your parents are divorced and one of them is getting remarried. And what's crazy is that Tamora isn't even romantically involved with my dad.

Ack, I better stop talking before I make myself vomit.

My brothers sat on a bench outside the condo near a fountain burbling water. A trio of stone mermaids frolicked in the fountain's center, frozen in poses reminding me of Disney's *The Little Mermaid*. I'm not sure how long the boys had been waiting, but when they saw me, Zac jumped to his feet and Jason smiled.

Zac ran to embrace me. "Maddie!"

I squeezed him tight. "Goodness, you act like an assassin was out to get me."

"One kinda was."

I ruffled his curly hair. "Yeah, but those jerkweeds can't catch me. You okay?"

He nodded.

Jason stood and stretched. "We were beginning to worry," he said. "How'd you lose the goon—" his eyes darted to my paint-splattered clothes. "What the heck happened to you?"

"I ran into an artist."

Jason shook his head. "Well, there's a shower and a change of clothes upstairs."

I glanced at the condo looming over us, its glass windows reflecting the blue sky and clouds like a mirror. "Is Tamora home?"

"Working," said Jason. "We should have enough time to clean up and look over the map before she returns."

Good. The last thing I needed was Tamora catching me. I figured once she found out I'd fled the hospital she'd send me back for sure. And I couldn't help Dad from a recovery bed.

The three of us approached the condo's entrance. A doorman in a black suit and tie greeted us. He opened one of the glass doors embossed with fancy lettering that read: THE PLAZA. His eyes lingered on me and my painted clothes.

"Don't worry," I teased. "I don't plan on blowing up anything today."

His shoulders relaxed.

I knew what he must be thinking: Oh, great, there's the girl who dropped a cherry bomb in the trash compactor. Have you ever seen garbage coating the walls and ceiling? I don't think the doorman had, either.

Once inside, cold air-conditioning felt refreshing and crisp. Classical music soothed from overhead speakers. My Converse high-tops and the boys' tennis shoes squeaked across the spacious lobby floor, its marble tiles black and gold. We reached the elevator doors. Zac hit the button. We waited, and none of us spoke. The doors opened up . . .

. . . and my stomach lurched.

Standing inside the elevator was an attractive woman in her early forties. Her blond hair was in an updo and lazy ringlets fell to her shoulders. A diamond necklace graced her slender neckline. She wore a white blouse with khaki pants and high heels.

"Maddie Jones," grinned Tamora Rose, but it wasn't a friendly smile—more like a shark showing teeth before devouring its prey. "You're in a world of trouble, young lady."

Chapter 19

"TAMORA, IT'S NOT WHAT YOU think," I attempted to explain. We now sat on a firm and uncomfortable leather sofa in Tamora's high-rise condominium. The place was ultra-modern, completely different from my house in the suburbs. Filled with things Tamora had collected on digs, the African pottery and Incan artifacts meshed well with her sleek furniture. Everything in the place looked stylish—magazine ready—but it lacked the warmth of a practical home.

"Imagine my surprise," Tamora said in her haughty British accent while she paced the living room floor. Behind her, floor-to-ceiling windows looked out on a city skyline. A late afternoon sun painted the town orange and red. "When I arrived at the hospital to find you kids missing. Do you have any idea how worried I've been?"

She looked at us as if expecting a response, but I only sniffled. The boys sat on my left and right and stared forward with blank faces.

"Ugh," she threw up her hands. "How'd you sneak out of the hospital, anyway?"

Despite my attempt to hide it, a smirk touched my lips. "The fire escape."

"Wow, just wow—" she pinched the bridge of her nose. "That was real stupid, Maddie. Did falling five floors not once cross your mind?"

"It crossed mine," Jason spoke up.

"Of course it did," Tamora said. She looked at Zac. "And what about you?"

Zac's smile stretched from ear to ear. "Coolest thing I've done all week."

Tamora shook her head. "Unbelievable. All right, we're heading back to the hospital. Let's hope I can convince the doctors and police this is all a big misunderstanding."

I gulped. Not good. More than likely the police at Dad's museum had seen the security footage by now. And if so, then I might as well kiss my hopes of helping Dad goodbye. They'd lock me up and throw away the key.

"You can't do that, Tamora," I said.

"Give me one good reason why?"

"Do you remember your dig in Ecuador?"

"Of course I do," she said. "What's your point?"

"My dad told me a story about a death-defying escape. He said the two of you excavated a burial mound—a site believed to be the resting place of an Incan mummy king. If I remember correctly, a tribe of local Indians attacked and you had to run away."

"Are you seriously comparing my escape to yours, Maddie? Because that was different. The natives chased us with poisonous blow darts."

"And we were chased by goons with poisonous cinnamon rolls."

She arched a heavily manicured eyebrow. "What?"

I explained how I ended up in the hospital, who the dead soldiers near Detective Murphy's blown-up car were, about the people with tattooed hands, everything.

"So we can't go back to the hospital," I said. "Rico's goons or the tattooed assassins might kill us. Our best option is to hide out here until things smooth over."

Tamora sat down in a zebra-print chair and sighed heavily. She glanced at a framed picture resting on a coffee table nearby and picked it up. The photograph was of a teenage boy of about nineteen years. His black hair was shaggy yet stylish, and as he leaned against a beautiful oak tree, his arms were folded across his chest. Tamora stared at the boy in the photograph, and a hint of sadness touched her eyes. I looked away, knowing Tamora's son died when I was only three years old.

"Tamora . . ." I said after a few moments. "What are you thinking?"

"I think you're a knucklehead, love."

"I mean about our situation."

"Well," she set the picture frame gently back on the coffee table. "Your father is missing. You believe people are out to get you. So . . . yeah . . . you kids are staying here tonight."

I sighed in relief.

Dried paint still clung to my skin and hair. Body odor drifted beneath my nose, and I felt confident the smell wasn't from my brothers. I stood, ready to hit the bathroom and take a hot shower, but my belly growled loudly.

Tamora glanced my way. "I've got a pizza in the freezer if you're hungry. Pepperoni, I believe."

Oh, man, a slice of pie sounded like heaven.

"And while you're eating—" she stood and headed to the kitchen to grab the pizza from the fridge. "You can tell me why you threw a brick into a museum window today."

Crap. Busted.

Chapter 20

LATER THAT NIGHT, AFTER WE'D eaten and showered (and lied to Tamora about the museum incident), I sprawled on a pallet of blankets on the living room floor. Jason lounged on the sofa. Zac was tucked in bed in the guest room—he'd called dibs and Tamora wasn't able to resist his baby-faced charm.

What a dingus.

Tamora stood in the kitchen with a view of all three of us. "You kids need anything before I head to bed?"

"Nope," I said.

"Think we're good," Jason added.

She turned off the lights. As soon as her bedroom door closed, I reached beneath my pillow and pulled out the map we'd found in Dad's office.

"Is it clear?" Zac whispered from the room.

"Yeah."

Jason threw off his blankets and sat beside me on the floor. Zac tip-toed into the living room and joined us. I unfolded the map carefully, afraid the soft and brittle parchment might crumble apart in my hands. Dim moonlight filtered through the condo's windows. It wasn't enough light to see the map's details, so Jason grabbed his phone and turned on its flashlight.

Zac gasped. "Whoa, it's a labyrinth of some kind."

He was right. The map showed a maze of tunnels all leading to a central circle. Chinese writing marked various passageways, but the ancient script was faded. Not that I could read it even if it was legible. I'm not bilingual or anything. But here and there, notes written in English were scratched along the edges.

Notes written in Dad's handwriting.

"Pit One has 6,000 warriors," Jason read aloud. "There are eleven corridors, but seek the seventh. Seven rows back, middle soldier."

"Sounds like directions," I said.

Jason nodded. He kept reading: "All terracotta warriors were given a stamp, a signature, but one warrior is unique. He is called the Shoemaker."

"The Shoemaker?"

Jason shrugged. "Beats me."

"Hey, what's that?" Zac pointed at the sketch of a single terracotta warrior drawn beside the labyrinthine tunnels.

"Looks like a diagram," said Jason.

"Beware," I read a note in the bottom right corner. "Do not open the tomb. The First Qin Emperor is cursed—"

Lights flickered on. I nearly jumped out of my skin.

"What are you kids doing?" Tamora stood near a light switch overlooking the living room with both hands on her hips.

I tucked the map beneath my leg. "Erm, we couldn't sleep."

"I see that. What are you *doing*?"

Jason cleared his throat. "Talking about Dad."

"Oh," Tamora's tone softened. "Well, get to bed. There's nothing you can do for him tonight."

Jason and Zac went to their sleeping spaces—one on the couch, the other in the guest bedroom. Tamora said goodnight, then she flicked off the lights. I settled into my pallet, but my mind raced with Dad's cryptic words. What did he mean?

"We found your map, Dad," I whispered into the dark. "Curse or no curse, we're coming to get you."

Around three o'clock in the morning, I heard sniffling coming from Zac's bedroom. He was crying. Hearing his sadness made my heart ache. Zac was the strongest kid I knew, but his sobs reminded me how young he really was. Man, somebody take a knife and—

Stab.

Twist.

Rip my heart out while you're at it.

Zac's crying was like icing on the frigging cake, a final note to end a rotten day. I wished Mom were still alive. She would crawl into bed with Zac and comfort him. But she wasn't with us anymore. No matter how badly I wanted to change the past, or how angry I got that she died when I was little, nothing would bring her back. And with Dad missing, that meant it was up to me to be there for Zac—for Jason, too, even if he pretended he was fine. I knew deep down he felt the same emotions I did.

Heartbroken. Scared. Confused.

I threw off my blanket and went to Zac's room. I snuggled into bed beside him, and he rolled over and hugged me. He kept weeping. I squeezed him.

"*Shhh*," I said. "It's gonna be okay. We'll figure this out."

But my mind raced with thoughts of Dad. I wondered where in the world he was right then, at this very moment, as I held onto my little brother for dear life. I remembered my last conversation with him, and how he gave me words of encouragement to tackle the rock wall. I often confided in Dad when things got me down.

The fact that he was gone suddenly hit me hard. Dad was really missing. I wouldn't see him when I woke up. And I had no idea when, or if I'd ever, see him again.

Tears blurred my vision. I swallowed down a sob. Zac needed me to be strong.

"What are we going to do?" he whispered.

I sighed, trying desperately to keep my breath from quivering. "We're going to get Dad back," I promised.

Chapter 21

I HAD ANOTHER DREAM.

This time I wasn't in a tomb. I stood on the rooftop of a hundred-story skyscraper while heavy rain blew sideways. Lightning flashed. The rest of the city came into view. Not Evansville. The sprawl was different: modern skyscrapers mixed with ancient Chinese architecture. Several buildings' rooftops flared at the corners.

Behind me, I heard a scream, but not like in horror flicks, more like in war movies when a soldier shouts a battle cry. I whirled around. Two men were fighting. But they weren't *men*. One was a mummy wrapped in tattered cloth, the other a terracotta warrior made of hardened clay. Each time lightning flashed, I saw them grappling with each other, wrestling, kicking, and head-butting. Thunder boomed, and it synced perfectly with one of their punches. Every hit tore away cloth or chipped away clay, revealing the decaying flesh of grotesque corpses.

Over the roar of wind and rain, I heard the mummy yelling at the terracotta warrior: *"Stop the nightmares! Release me!"*

"Never!" the terracotta warrior shouted.

The rain got worse, pelting me, soaking my clothes. A rumble came from somewhere high above. I turned toward the city. The beginnings of a tornado formed in the sky. It was massive. Blood-red light illuminated swirling clouds.

The mummy crooned, its voice so cold it turned my blood to ice. *"Stop the nightmares, please!"*

"No!" the terracotta warrior yelled.

The wind became a squall. It whipped around making my clothes flutter and snap. The tornado touched down—

—and a meteor blasted from the clouds.

It struck the city. A thunderous explosion sounded. Fire and black smoke engulfed the sky. The blast sent me flying. I tumbled over the edge of the skyscraper and fell. The ground rushed up to meet me. I screamed and flailed as the wind rushed by, but right before I struck the ground . . .

Chapter 22

I WOKE UP.

The strange sensation of falling still lingered. I glanced around and noticed I was in the same place where I'd fallen asleep—in Zac's bed in the guest room. My body felt like it neared midnight, but gray sunlight illuminated Tamora's condo. Thunder rolled across the city. A storm was brewing. I hadn't dreamed that.

I rolled over and saw Zac's side of the bed was nothing but crumpled sheets. It appeared even at Tamora's place he was an early riser. A sizzling sound came from the kitchen. The smell of bacon filled my nostrils.

"Rise and shine, Maddie Jones," Tamora's voice called from the kitchen. "Breakfast is ready!"

Groggy, I crawled out of bed and put on nearly the same clothes as yesterday: blue jeans with rips in the knees and my dark denim jacket with the built-in hoodie (now splattered with bits of dry paint). I wore a different graphic Tee underneath, though. This one depicted a yellow happy face with crossed-out eyes and the word Nirvana.

I walked out of the guest room and made my way to a barstool. The spread Tamora had prepared looked delicious: scrambled eggs, English muffins, and, of course, crisp bacon. She set a plate of food down in front of me.

"Where are the boys?" I asked, scraping a bite of eggs into my mouth with an oversized fork.

Tamora put on earrings, already dressed in fashionable pants and a blouse. "Zac is downstairs exercising in the condo's gym. And Jason—he's calling your dad."

"W-what?" I choked on a bite of English muffin smeared with butter and strawberry jam.

"I've been trying to call him." Jason appeared from the hallway with his phone pressed to his ear. "But it keeps going to voicemail."

"Oh, for a second I thought—"

"Nobody's heard from him if that's what you're hoping." Jason pocketed his phone and grabbed a plate of food. He sat beside me at the bar.

Tamora shouldered her purse. "Okay, kids, I'm heading to work. No leaving the apartment today. Understood?"

I shoved a bite of bacon into my mouth. Its saltiness tasted like heaven.

"Maddie?" Tamora eyed me. "I mean it."

I put my hands up. "Hey, you know me. I can follow simple instructions."

"Mm-hmm." She headed for the door. "I may be late getting home. The museum called, and they asked me to approve a shipment of mummies headed to China since your dad is unavailable."

I scoffed. "Seriously? Dad's missing and that's their concern?"

"Hey, I get it, love. But the museum's Board of Directors insists on showing China their appreciation for the terracotta warriors they sent."

I stopped chewing at the sound of *terracotta warriors*.

"I should be home before bedtime. There's food in the pantry if you kids get hungry. Just clean the kitchen when you're done."

"Will do," Jason said. "Breakfast is delicious."

Tamora smiled. She closed the door behind her and left.

I finished the last of my bacon, but I didn't notice its flavor because something else now occupied my mind. Tamora's comment about the terracotta warriors reminded me of Detective Murphy's black and white surveillance photographs. Rico Raja approached my dad on the same day the terracotta warriors arrived at the museum. Why?

"Jason," I set my fork down on my plate. "Can you look up something on your phone?"

Jason swallowed a bite of eggs. "Erm, sure," he wiped his mouth with a napkin. "What'd you need?"

"Search for Rico Raja. See if there are news stories about him from the past twenty-four hours."

"Didn't we do that already?"

"We did, but now I've got a hunch."

If Rico was interested in the terracotta warriors here in Evansville, then he'd likely be interested in the main exhibit overseas in China. And a guy like Rico likely didn't travel without some sort of media attention. Jason pulled his phone from his pocket and opened a web browser. As he searched online, I took another bite of English muffin, then pushed my plate aside.

The front door opened. Zac walked in. A towel was draped across his shoulders and he glistened with sweat. "Hey, guys," he said, closing the door. "What you doing?"

"About to watch a video," Jason said, propping his phone up on a glass of orange juice.

"You found something?" I asked.

"CNN aired a story last night."

Zac grabbed a protein smoothie from the fridge and joined us at the bar. Jason hit play, and we huddled together to watch the tiny screen.

"*Ortega Industries is traveling to China,*" a blond anchorwoman began, sitting behind a desk in a studio newsroom. "*The company's CEO, Rico Raja, has a passion for history and he's interested in visiting the Tomb of the First Qin Emperor—the site of the greatest archaeological discovery of the 20th Century, the extraordinary terracotta army. The Chinese government is excited to play host to such a successful businessman.*"

Of course they are, I thought. Detective Murphy said Rico was likely conducting shady weapons deals beneath the U.S. government's nose.

Video footage of a landing strip appeared onscreen while text scrolled across the bottom. A private jet was parked on the tarmac. The anchorwoman went on to talk about Ortega Industry's humble beginnings in the midnineties, its booming growth in the past decade, and Rico's takeover of the company, but I was no longer focused on her words. Instead, my attention was solely on the footage being shown.

A retinue of men boarded the plane. They all looked like ex-soldiers: buzz cuts, strong jaws, and determined. One of them wore an eyepatch and had a nasty scar across his cheek. I chuckled at seeing my handy work. Juggernaut goons should think twice before messing with my Three Stooges fighting style.

A bald man stepped into view. He was as big as an NFL linebacker, more mercenary than fat rich man, and he wore an expensive Armani suit. His nationality might've been Middle-Eastern based on his skin tone and dark eyebrows. I recognized his profile from Detective Murphy's black and white photographs.

Rico Raja.

I gritted my teeth. I was convinced Rico had kidnapped Dad. He needed to pay.

"Maddie, are you okay?" asked Zac. "You look like you're ready to step into a boxing ring."

"No, things are *not* okay," I spat. "Dad could be on that plane right now bound and gagged."

Everyone boarded. All except Rico and a single companion. They spoke privately. The companion had an athletic build and black hair tucked behind pierced ears. He placed a hand on Rico's shoulder, and I noticed a tattoo.

"Holy crap, that's him!" I shouted.

"Who?" asked Jason.

"The guy who burglarized Dad's office. Standing beside Rico."

News footage went back to the anchorwoman at her desk. She was wrapping up the story.

"Rewind it," I said.

"What's the point?" said Zac. "We saw what the guy looks like."

"Just do it!"

Jason picked up his phone and rewound the footage.

"Stop," I said. "Pause on the image showing the tattoo."

He did. The video froze, its high-definition image paused on the moment the man with the tattooed hand touched Rico's shoulder. The tattoo was clearly visible. I studied it. It wasn't tribal. It was definitely a Chinese letter.

"Hang on a sec." Jason swiped to a new screen and opened a new app, but I couldn't keep up with the programs he accessed.

"What are you doing?" I asked.

"Running a Google image search."

"You can do that?"

"Of course." He typed with his thumbs and swiped to another screen. "Bingo! The tattoo is hànzì—a character from the Chinese alphabet. Unlike our English language, hànzì can represent more than simple sounds—they can express ideas or concepts. And that tattoo represents . . ." he paused, his expression grim.

"What is it?"

"It's a symbol of the Chinese Triad, what we here in America refer to as the Mafia."

"You've got to be kidding," I groaned. What was an American businessman doing with a dangerous gangster? And to think, I didn't believe things could get any worse. Boy, was I wrong.

Chapter 23

A STRANGE FEELING UNSETTLED MY stomach. It wasn't anger or anticipation or a desire for revenge. It was fear. Rico had tried to kidnap or kill me several times so far, with the car accident, the poisoned hospital food, and the scarred Juggernaut goon. My dad was missing because of *him* . . . and now he was flying to China to visit the terracotta warriors.

I wanted to run and hide. Rico's soldiers looked like they ate nails for breakfast and asked for seconds. But if my father was on that plane . . .

Zac was trembling. His hands were balled into fists. "We have to go after them."

"What?" I said. "Go after Rico?"

"Yeah," he said. "If he kidnapped Dad, and now he's leaving the country, and the cops can't do anything . . ." Tears streaked down his cheeks.

"He's right," Jason said. "We're gonna have to fly to China and bust some heads."

"Do you guys hear yourselves?" I said. "Rico is the head of a weapons manufacturing company. He has soldiers— and now the Chinese Triad is involved. If we went after them it would be suicide."

"But we have to do *something!*"

"Like what? We're kids. They're adults. And they have guns for crying out loud."

"C'mon, Maddie." Jason pushed back from the bar and stood. "All those pranks you do, dodging the police and risking your neck—but now Dad's in trouble and you won't even budge?"

My stomach lurched. "Those pranks are just jokes, Jason. No one died when I toilet papered city hall. And the only neck I'm risking is mine. But now . . . you guys are involved. And if something happened to one of you . . ."

"Dad's the one you should be worried about, Maddie. Not us."

"So let me get this straight," I said. "We're supposed to fly to China and confront one of the most powerful men in the world?"

"Yes," he said.

"Find Rico and stop him from doing whatever it is he has planned with the terracotta warriors?"

"Yes."

"And rescue Dad in the process?"

"That's about right."

I scoffed.

"China might be very nice this time of year?" Zac added weakly, as though *that* would convince me.

I didn't say anything.

Emotions rolled around inside me like bits of glass in a washing machine. I didn't know whether I felt angry or bitter or uncertain or sad. But I knew which emotion felt stronger than the rest.

I was afraid.

Afraid of losing Dad. Afraid of confronting the men who kidnapped him. Afraid of getting hurt or my brothers being killed.

Jason eyed me over the rims of his black glasses. "Look," he said. "We can't ask you to come with us. But Zac and I . . . we're not backing down."

Zac crossed his arms, a look of determination in his blue eyes.

I sighed. My breath quivered on the exhale. "Here's the deal, guys," I said. "What you're proposing is beyond dangerous. It's suicidal. But if . . . if you're serious about going . . . then I won't let you down."

They both smiled.

I stood from the bar and hugged them. My brothers meant more to me than any friend I'd ever had. Their determination to save our father made me love them even more. I wasn't sure what the three of us could do against Rico's forces, but I felt better knowing my brothers would be with me.

Zac released our hug. "There's just one problem."

"What?" I asked.

"How the heck do we get to China?"

Chapter 24

"MUMMIES," I SAID.

"Excuse me?" said Jason.

"Tamora mentioned a crate of mummies being shipped to China today. We can stow away with the cargo."

"Is that even possible?" asked Zac.

"No," Jason said. "We'd be breaking about a hundred laws."

"Since when have rules stopped us before?" I asked.

"That's beside the point."

"Do you have a better idea?" I walked around the bar and set my dirty plate in the kitchen sink. "Because last time I checked, you need a visa and passport to travel overseas."

Jason sighed. "Okay, you're right, we don't have many options. But what about food, water, clothes, and money for the journey?"

"We can bring those items with us," I said, rinsing my plate and loading it into the dishwasher. "We have clothes, there's plenty of food in Tamora's pantry, and I saw bottled waters at the bottom of the fridge. As for money, well, we have the Chinese currency we got from Dad's office. What did you call them?"

"Renminbi," said Jason. "Or yuan."

"Right, so money's not an issue."

"You're forgetting something."

"What?"

"Airport security," Jason said. "All passengers and their luggage are X-rayed to prevent terrorists from taking over planes. This means cargo planes will have their shipments X-rayed, too."

"Well . . ." I said slowly, thinking. "Then airport security will X-ray the crate and see bones—our bones—but they'll think they're seeing mummy bones. We'll just have to be really still."

"What about the mummies already in the crate? Don't you think security will get suspicious if they see half a dozen skeletons inside?"

"Hmmm," I said. "Then we'll have to remove the mummies at the museum before Tamora signs off on her paperwork."

Zac scoffed. "Remove the mummies? Where the heck will we put them?"

"I dunno." I dried my wet hands on a towel. "We'll have to stash them out of sight somewhere."

He shook his head, unconvinced.

"Look," I slapped the counter and pointed at the boys. "You guys want to save Dad, right? That means we must do something drastic if we're going to reach China. Shipping ourselves as mummies is our best option."

"It is a decent idea," Jason said.

"Of course it is," I said. "Now let's get our butts to the museum before Tamora does."

Chapter 25

IT WAS STORMING WHEN WE arrived at the museum. I shut the door of the taxi and huddled beneath a large black umbrella with Jason and Zac as the cabby drove away. Rain pattered, and despite Jason's efforts to keep us all covered, my shoes were soaked in a matter of seconds. A flash of lightning streaked across the sky followed by a crack of thunder. I didn't know if the weather was a bad omen or what.

"This may be more difficult than we thought," said Jason. "The crate of mummies may already be on that truck."

An eighteen-wheeler was parked in the loading dock behind the museum. Three workers in rain gear loaded wooden crates into the truck's trailer. The museum's warehouse door was up, a rolling door that could easily fit two cars. Yellow light illuminated its entrance.

I shouldered a backpack full of items we thought essential for the trip: clothes, bottled water, snacks we'd raided from Tamora's pantry, Dad's map, and the Chinese money. "We need a distraction."

"Like what?"

"Dunno," I said as thunder rumbled. "But those workers will make finding the crate of mummies difficult."

"I have an idea," said Zac. "Follow my lead."

"What? Wait—"

Zac stepped clear of our umbrella and into the heavy downpour. He ran across the parking lot and darted for the eighteen-wheeler.

"What's he doing?" Jason mumbled.

"Something stupid," I said.

Zac reached the truck's driver-side door. He opened it and clambered inside.

"Definitely something stupid," I said. "He's gonna drive the truck."

"What? No way!"

Head bowed, I darted into the downpour. The rain felt like an icy waterfall emptied onto my head. My compass necklace bounced on my chest as I sprinted across the parking lot. I tried to hurry to avoid getting wet, but I was drenched by the time I reached the front of the eighteen-wheeler. I leaned against its grill. Rain blurred my vision.

BEEEEEP! The truck's horn blared.

The noise startled me. I flinched and held my ears. This close to the truck the horn was an earsplitting screech. Heart racing, I peeked around the headlights to find the dock workers—but their gazes snapped toward the truck. I leaned back against the grill hoping they didn't see me. The horn stopped blaring.

"What was that?!" one of the dock workers shouted.

"The truck!" another yelled.

"Somebody's in the truck?!"

Boots stomped toward the eighteen-wheeler's cab, splashing as the dock workers ran into the rain. It sounded like the workers were scrambling to the truck's driver's side door.

Jason grabbed me by the shoulder and whirled me around. He no longer held the umbrella. He must've tossed it so he wouldn't be easily spotted. His spiky blond hair was wet and flat on top of his head. "Follow me," he mouthed.

Crouching low, I followed Jason around the truck's passenger side. When we stepped past the passenger door, Zac popped it open and slipped outside.

"I tried to drive it," he said, "but I couldn't reach the pedals."

"Well, the horn worked," I said. "C'mon!"

We made it to the back of the eighteen-wheeler's trailer. A glance inside told me the crate of mummies hadn't been loaded yet. The crates stacked inside the trailer were no bigger than moving boxes.

A gruff voice drew my attention: "Must've been a glitch in the truck's system."

"Not surprised. The electronics have been faulty for years."

Oh, fetch! The workers were coming back.

"Quick, get inside," I said.

The three of us darted into the museum's warehouse through the open door. Yellow light temporarily blinded us after coming in from the gloomy weather, but we quickly bounded left and hid behind a stack of crates. Looking around, I saw a dozen more crates ready to be loaded. And right in the middle of the loading area was a crate the size of a sarcophagus. It could hold a trio of mummies, easy.

A streak of lightning flashed. Thunder boomed as a dock worker emerged inside the warehouse. His yellow raincoat dripped water. "Guys, I'm gonna check the weather radar," he said, his voice gruff. "This storm is brutal."

"Wait up," said a second worker in a red raincoat. His shoes squished as he walked into the warehouse and his coat glistened in the light. "I could use a cup of coffee to warm me up."

They exited through a hallway door, leaving one remaining dock worker behind. The worker took off his red raincoat and hung it on a hook near a door labeled BATHROOM. He opened the door and slipped inside. The loading area was now empty.

"Now's our chance. Go!"

We rushed to the wooden crate of mummies, not knowing if we had one minute or ten. The crate was nailed shut. I jammed my fingers into a slight crack and pulled, but I couldn't pry the lid open.

"We need a hammer or pry bar," breathed Jason.

"Search," I whispered.

We went in three directions. I ran to a red toolbox, Jason darted to a shelf of assorted items, and Zac hurried to a wall with random tools hanging on hooks. The toolbox's top drawer was locked so I tried the next drawer. Locked. I tried opening the other drawers, too—also locked. Crap! I whirled around searching for anything useful. Time was ticking. The dock workers could return any second.

"I found one!" Zac ran back to the crate of mummies holding a pry bar in his hand. Jason and I rushed to join him.

He wedged the pry bar beneath the lid and pulled down with all of his weight, but the nails wouldn't budge.

"Yes, Miss Rose, the crate of mummies will be loaded next."

"Good, they must reach Xi'an no later than tomorrow evening."

Oh, my God! That sounded like Tamora and the dock worker with a gruff voice. Their voices came from the other side of the hallway door, and they sounded close.

"Just a moment," I heard Tamora say. "Let me look over the paperwork again."

I scrambled to Zac, shoved him aside, and jumped on top of the pry bar. My heavier weight did the trick. The lid came loose. I used the pry bar to loosen a few more nails, then we popped the wooden lid off completely. Inside, three mummies rested on a bed of straw lying side by side, wrapped in bandages that must've been thousands of years old.

"Grab a mummy," I instructed, and we each reached inside and hoisted a corpse.

Gross doesn't begin to describe what I felt as I ran with a dead body thrown over my shoulder. Sick might be a better word. I was surprised to find the mummy didn't stink. It just smelled musty, like something extremely old. I guess since all of its internal organs had been removed long ago there wasn't a stench of decay. Good for me.

But as I reached an empty crate and tucked the mummy inside, its head fell off. My cheeks puffed as I nearly vomited. Luckily, bandages kept the head from rolling away. I picked up the head and set it back onto the mummy.

"Sorry," I breathed, covering the crate with a lid. Then I rushed back to the crate we needed to hide inside. The boys reached the crate at the same time, having hidden their mummies in different places inside the warehouse. I didn't see their mummies from here, and that was good enough for me.

The toilet flushed.

"Crap—go, go, go!"

We tossed our backpacks into the crate and hopped inside. I slid the lid over us, lining up the nails with their nail holes, and it settled back into place just as the bathroom and hallway doors opened. We froze in place and did our best to keep our breathing steady.

Chapter 26

I HEARD FOOTSTEPS APPROACHING the crate, and Tamora's British accent. "Oh, this is just rubbish. You didn't close the crate properly."

"What?" said the dock worker with a gruff voice. "I nailed the lid shut this morning."

"Does this look secure to you?"

Heavy thuds sounded as the dock worker came closer to inspect, his work boots stomping with each stride. I crossed my fingers and prayed our flight to China wasn't about to end before it ever got started. "What the hell? The nails are all popped off."

Jason touched my arm and pointed. I looked to where he motioned. A shaft of yellow light filtered inside the crate at the corner. Through the gap, I could see Tamora's white blouse and the buttons on the dock worker's yellow raincoat. For the briefest second, Tamora's face flashed by and I thought she saw me hiding inside—but she didn't raise any alarms and the dock worker continued speaking.

"Joe, grab a pair of hammers, would ya? Let's lift this lid and realign it."

Oh, no! They were going to find us.

"You needn't bother," said Tamora. Something heavy pressed down on the lid's corner where it was cracked open, shutting the crate completely and thrusting us into darkness. "I need this crate loaded. Now. It must reach China by the appointed time."

"Yes, ma'am."

Hammers pounded as the nails were all secured. Then the crate jerked forward. The workers must've been pushing the crate toward the eighteen-wheeler's trailer because I felt the surface beneath me vibrating with each push. I heard the sound of wood scraping against concrete. I set a hand on my backpack to steady myself as I knelt in the straw. Any change in the cargo's weight might draw unwanted attention.

The crate stopped moving. I heard the trailer door slam closed, the eighteen-wheeler's engine crank, and I think we started moving as the truck pulled away from the museum. It felt like we were picking up speed. Tires roared on asphalt as the eighteen-wheeler rumbled down the road.

I leaned against the wall of the crate and heaved a sigh. It was too dark to see my brothers.

"I can't believe that worked," whispered Zac.

"It nearly didn't," Jason said.

"We got lucky," I said. "Tamora nearly saw me."

"The airport is a short drive from the museum," Jason said. I heard him shifting straw around even though I couldn't see him. "We need to lie down like mummies."

"Right," I said, and I did what he suggested.

The straw felt itchy against my skin. It poked and prodded, and I tried my best to ignore the itching sensations. If we didn't prepare ourselves to be extremely still, our plan wouldn't work.

Thirty minutes later, the eighteen-wheeler slowed to a stop. The trailer door opened. Footsteps sounded as workers began unloading crates. I inhaled deeply and tried to calm my nerves. The trickiest part—lying completely still while airport security X-rayed the crate—could make or break our flight.

We started moving again. The crate scraped the ground and our bodies jostled around despite our attempts to keep still. I could hear workers grunting as they pushed us forward. Then, quite unexpectedly, we were going down quickly as though we were on a slide. My tummy fluttered like it does when riding roller coasters, but then we leveled out. Now we surged forward, not by the strength of workers, but by what felt like the movement of conveyor belts.

Suddenly, we stopped.

"What'd you have for me today?" said a sassy woman's voice.

"Mummies," replied the gruff voice I recognized as the dock worker from the museum.

"Yuck," said the woman. "All right, let me get my scanner."

Seconds later, I heard *beeps* and *boops* and knew this was it. The crate was being X-rayed. Holding my breath, I froze like a statue. Then—

"What on earth," the woman said.

"What?" said the dock worker.

"These skeletons—they're really small. Were they children or something?"

"Maybe. The Egyptians were smaller than we are today."

More *beeps* and *boops*, and—

"Oh, my word . . ."

"What now?" said the dock worker in an impatient voice.

"Is that your phone?"

"Excuse me?"

"Look, there's a phone lying next to one of the mummies."

The dock worker groaned. "My partner must've dropped it when loading the mummies. If you'll give me a moment I can open the crate and—"

"Sir," the woman said. "If you dropped your phone you'll have to buy a replacement—because you are *not* opening this thing up in here."

"Why not?"

"Haven't you heard of King Tut?"

"King Tut?"

"The cursed mummy," she said. "Nearly all the people who opened his tomb died of mysterious causes. Everybody knows that. So if you think you're gonna open a crate of curses up in here, you'd best think again."

"Fine," the dock worker said. "So is the crate clear to fly?"

"Oh, it's clear. And I'm gonna make sure we load these mummies on the plane straightaway—because I don't need no curses in my warehouse."

The crate started moving again, and I finally released my breath, exhaling deeply.

"Sorry," Jason whispered. "My phone must've slipped out of my bag."

"No worries," I breathed. "But keep quiet—at least until we're in the air."

Another hour went by. The crate finally stopped being moved from place to place. The noise of jet engines eventually drowned out all sound, and we felt the speed of flight as the plane rumbled down the tarmac right before it lifted from the ground.

Finally, we were on our way to China.

Chapter 27

WHEN I THOUGHT THE COAST was clear, we kicked the crate's lid up and peeked around. We were on a plane all right, in what looked like the inside of a cargo hold. Crates, boxes, and countless suitcases filled the cabin. No sentries appeared to be standing guard, so we climbed out of the crate and stretched.

Zac yawned. "Man, my back hurts. How long have we been in there?"

"About three hours." Jason sat down with his back propped against the crate. He unzipped a backpack and pulled out a bottle of water, uncapped it, and took a big swig. "And we still have a long way to go. China is about a twelve-hour flight, assuming we don't have layovers."

I sat beside Jason and wriggled my toes to get the blood flowing. My tummy growled. I still had a few snacks inside my backpack: pretzels, Ritz crackers, and fruit. I took out the pretzels, popped one into my mouth, and tried to blink the weariness from my eyes. Lying in a dark crate for several hours had made me sleepy.

Zac motioned to the cargo. "What is all this stuff?"

"Imports and exports," said Jason, taking another swig of water. "America sends goods to China, and we get all those 'Made in China' products." He looked at me. "What's the plan for when we land?"

I crunched into another salty pretzel. "I have no idea."

"Please tell me you're joking."

"Hey, I've never done this before. I'm making it up as we go."

Jason groaned. He took out his cell phone and powered it on.

"Look, I'm sorry," I said. "I guess our next task is to sneak out of the airport without getting caught."

"And after that?" Zac called as he explored the maze of crates.

"We'll need a hotel room." Jason opened his phone's web browser. "It looks like I can access the plane's Wi-Fi. Give me a moment to find hotels around Xi'an."

"Xi'an?" I repeated.

"It's the city Tamora said the mummies are being shipped to."

For the next few hours, Jason busied himself on his phone. Zac wandered around the cargo hold searching the maze of boxes and crates, but he eventually got bored and sat down beside me. He rested his head on my shoulder and drifted off to sleep. Meanwhile, my mind raced with random ideas of what to do next.

Sure, we needed a hotel room so we could recover from jet lag, but there was also a big question mark about what to do after we rested. When we hastily planned this trip in Tamora's kitchen, the boys had spoken like warriors who could defeat the bad guys in a single blow. But what could the three of us really do against a guy like Rico?

One step at a time, Maddie, I told myself. *What would Dad do in a situation like this?*

He would do his homework, I realized. He'd learn all he could about Rico Raja, Ortega Industries, and the terracotta warriors. Then he'd plan his next move based on what he'd learned.

"Jason," I whispered, trying not to wake Zac. "Can you find out where the Museum of Terracotta Warriors is located?"

"Sure," he said, rubbing his neck. "What are you thinking?"

"I think we need to scope out the place. Play tourist and take a tour. See if we can figure out what Rico is after. The news video we saw said Rico planned to visit the Tomb of the First Qin Emperor."

Jason nodded. "Good idea. Plus we have Dad's map."

"Exactly. Locating the Shoemaker should be a number one priority."

"The Shoemaker?"

"Dad's map mentioned something about it?"

"Oh, yeah."

I turned my attention to the surrounding cargo. The Pacific Ocean likely loomed 35,000 feet beneath us, but with no windows, it was hard to tell. I'd only seen the Pacific Ocean once when we had traveled to India on a family vacation a few years after Mom passed away. Although I had only been eight years old at the time, I still remembered how blue the ocean looked as I stared out my passenger seat window. The water had been so massive and powerful.

Much like the man who kidnapped Dad, I thought.

I shivered, even though I wasn't cold. From here on out, I got a feeling things were going to get sketchy.

Part Two

TOMB OF THE FIRST QIN EMPEROR

Chapter 28

A LOUD BANG STARTLED US.

The jet engines' roar changed pitch, and I realized the plane's landing gear must be lowering into place. It felt like the plane's speed was slowing down, too. We clambered back inside the crate, lowered the lid, and laid down in the straw. My stomach suddenly lurched as the plane tilted to the left. The pressure changed, and I swallowed several times trying to pop my ears. I knew from years of flying that when cabin pressure changed it meant the plane was lowering in altitude.

We were getting ready to land.

I wasn't sure how long we needed to hide inside the crate. Should we sneak out at the first available moment? Or wait until the crate was shipped to the museum? Although it would be cool if the crate was shipped directly to the Museum of Terracotta Warriors, we didn't know for sure if that's where the crate was heading. Besides, what we really needed was rest and food—other than pretzels, crackers, and fruit.

And we needed time to plan our next move.

Bouts of turbulence jostled us around. None of us spoke, but I could hear Zac breathing deeply. We'd once traveled on a plane with heavy turbulence—the plane had dropped twenty feet in the air—and Zac had never gotten over it. He still got nervous anytime planes shook and banked unexpectedly.

Thankfully, the turbulence subsided, and soon after I felt a sudden jolt and heard tires screeching as the plane touched down. The pilots hit the brakes, and I was thrown forward into my brothers.

"Ouch!" said Jason.

"Your elbow is in my neck!" said Zac.

"Sorry," I apologized, rolling back onto my side of the crate.

The plane slowed to a stop. We resettled ourselves in the straw and waited. It seemed like the plane was jockeying to a hangar where its cargo could be unloaded. Finally, I heard movement outside our crate. And talking. People speaking in Chinese. Then a hydraulic whining sounded which might've been the plane's cargo door opening.

Before long, our crate was being moved.

But we weren't moved very far because after a brief descent with the crate's floor rumbling beneath us, we stopped. The voices grew louder, but I couldn't understand them since they didn't speak English. Slowly, the voices faded out of earshot. Feeling brave, I got to my knees and lifted the lid slightly.

Bright sunlight stung my eyes. Squinting, I saw that our crate had come to rest on the tarmac outside of a large hangar. The plane's massive cargo door was lowered. Workers with black hair and blue jumpsuits climbed a ramp leading to the plane's cargo hold. They were unloading crates. I glanced left and right. No one else was around. If ever there was an opportunity to sneak away, this was it.

"Time to go, boys," I breathed, grabbing my bag.

"Really," said Zac, excited.

"Stay close. Keep low."

I shoved the lid off the crate and climbed out. The boys hopped out beside me. We lowered the lid back into place so the crate looked undisturbed, then we sprinted away from the cargo plane. Ahead, I could see the main airport building across the tarmac. I figured that's where we needed to go. From there, we could blend in with the crowd of travelers and disappear.

A luggage car went zooming past pulling several trailers filled with suitcases. We quickly jumped behind a stack of tires to hide. The driver didn't appear to see us. He drove toward a passenger jet fueling up for take-off.

"We can't go that way," I said.

"What about over there," Jason pointed.

My eyes scanned the area Jason motioned to. Behind the hangar loomed a chain-link fence. A sidewalk snaked its way beside it, leading to the airport's entrance where cars were parked, passengers unloaded their luggage, and a line of taxis waited to pick up fares.

"Jump the fence?" he suggested.

I nodded.

We raced for the fence before anyone could spot us. I crashed into it, stuck my fingers through its links, and climbed. I hopped over and landed on the other side, then looked around. To our left, tourists entered and exited the airport's main lobby, many pulling smart little suitcases on wheels. A shuttle bus drove by. Horns blared up and down the street. I glanced back at the hangar to see if any workers in blue jumpsuits chased us. They weren't. So I shouldered my bag and walked toward the throng of people in front of the airport. The boys fell in step beside me.

"I made a reservation online at the Shunda Hotel," said Jason. "I've got their address programmed into my phone."

"Great," I said. "Let's get a taxi and get out of here."

"Can you speak Mandarin?" asked Zac.

"No."

"Then how will we communicate with a driver? They might not speak English."

"We'll figure it out. One step at a time."

"Excuse me," someone tapped my shoulder, startling me. "Are you Maddie Jones?"

I turned to see an older man in a black suit and hat holding a cardboard sign. He wore dark sunglasses and his grin was framed by a bushy, gray mustache. He looked to be at least fifty years old.

I glanced down at his cardboard sign. It read: JONES FAMILY.

"I'm looking for three children," the man explained, his English accent sounding like his native tongue might be Mandarin. "I believe their names are Maddie, Jason, and Zac. Would you three be them?"

"Erm—" I didn't know what to say. Who knew we were coming? More importantly, what if this was one of Rico's traps?

"My client has arranged for their pick up," the man informed. "And she has reserved a room at the Angsana Xi'an Lintong."

"Dude," whispered Jason. "That's a five-star hotel. I saw it when looking for an affordable place to stay."

"Who is *she*?" I asked the man suspiciously.

"Why, Tamora Rose, of course," he replied. "She has been expecting your arrival."

Chapter 29

THE MAN'S CADILLAC LIMOUSINE WAS the nicest car I'd ever ridden in. It had black leather seats, chrome on nearly everything, a wide-screen TV, and neon lights along the floorboard. Despite its posh interior, the fresh scent of pine filled the air. A tree-shaped car freshener hung on an air vent.

Zac opened the mini-fridge and pulled out an ice-cold Coca-Cola. "I can't believe this is all free."

"For reals," mumbled Jason through a mouthful of Hershey's chocolate bar.

I gazed out the window at the sprawling cityscape. Xi'an was beautiful. Modern skyscrapers and traditional Chinese architecture blended with rolling hills in the background. In the middle of the city sat a huge bell tower, its green roof flaring at the corners with red pillars flanking its sides. Old city walls were still erected here and there, a testament to the ancient people who once lived here long ago.

"Are you guys not worried about Tamora?" I asked, bringing my attention back inside the limousine.

Zac shrugged. "What can she do? Tamora is on the other side of the world. At least this way we get to feel what it's like to be rich."

"You gotta admit this is pretty cool," said Jason. "We've never ridden in a limo before."

I shook my head and went back to staring out the window. I suddenly realized the city looked a lot like the one from my dream. It gave me an eerie feeling of déjà vu.

Jason noticed me admiring the scenery. "Xi'an is one of China's oldest cities," he said. "I learned about the place while researching on the plane. It once marked the eastern edge of the Silk Road—an ancient network of trade routes connecting Japan to the Mediterranean Sea. It was also the hometown of China's first emperor: Qin Shi Huang. That's why his tomb is here. The terracotta warriors were built to guard him in the afterlife."

"That's cool," I feigned interest.

"I know, right? The terracotta army is made up of all kinds of soldiers—"

The partition window separating us from the driver suddenly rolled down. "Tàitài Rose wishes to speak with you."

"What?" I asked.

"Tàitài means *Misses* in Mandarin," said Jason.

"Don't be such a nerd. I'm talking about Tamora."

The driver motioned to a phone beside the back window. Its red light blinked signaling somebody on hold. I eyed the phone nervously.

"Are you gonna answer it?" asked Zac.

"Why do I have to take the call?"

"Because you're the oldest," said Jason.

I rolled my eyes. Stupid scaredy-cats. They weren't afraid of Tamora a moment ago while enjoying refreshments on her dime. It looked like I was about to get my butt chewed out. There was no way I could avoid a conversation with Tamora now. She had caught us red-handed. So I inhaled deeply to try and calm my nerves, then I answered the call.

"Hello?"

"What the hell were you thinking?!"

I pulled the phone away from my ear, but Tamora yelled so loudly I could still hear her angry voice.

"I told you not to leave the apartment, and what'd you do? You hide in my shipment of mummies and leave the bloody country!"

Whoa, how'd she find out about that? "Tamora," I began.

"Don't even start, Maddie. Mr. Yao is taking you to the hotel—where I want you to stay. Do not leave the hotel room. Understand? I'm boarding first class now so I'll be there tomorrow to pick you kids up. And one more thing, the police have a warrant out for your arrest for breaking and entering the museum."

Eek, I thought. *That's a lot more serious than one of my pranks.*

Tamora scolded me for another five minutes. When her voice finally went hoarse, and she'd finished speaking her peace, I hung up the call.

"What'd she say?" asked Jason.

I pressed my forehead against the limousine's cold window and sighed. "That she's gonna kill us."

Chapter 30

IF I THOUGHT THE LIMOUSINE nice, it was nothing compared to the Angsana Xi'an Lintong hotel. The place had four restaurants, a full-service spa, and an indoor heated pool. Our room included a view of the city, a hot tub, and sleek furniture with decorations boasting an Asian flair.

I dropped my backpack on the bed and plopped down with a sigh. The bed felt soft and I sank into its thick comforter. I wanted nothing more than to curl up and sleep, but my belly growled. It had been hours since I'd last eaten the meager snack of pretzels on the plane.

Zac picked up a restaurant menu from one of the bedside tables. "Room service?"

"Is the Pope Catholic?" I asked.

He scrunched his brow in confusion.

"That means *yes*, doofus."

"Oh." He handed me the menu so I could glance it over. Most of the items were foreign. No American burgers or fries. Fine with me. I loved Chinese food. We placed an order: sweet-and-sour chicken, moo goo gai pan, Peking roasted duck, custard tarts, chocolate cake, fried ice cream, dragon's beard candy . . . all on Tamora's tab. They said the food would be delivered shortly.

Jason found an outlet and plugged in his phone so it could charge. "What's the plan for tomorrow?"

I unzipped my backpack and pulled out Dad's map. Even after hours spent studying it during the flight, the maze of tunnels still looked like a confusing mess. "We need to visit the Museum of Terracotta Warriors."

"Wait, so we're not staying in the hotel room like Tamora said?"

"What'd you think?"

Jason put his hands up. "Hey, I'm just checking."

"Guys, look at this." Zac held up a brochure he'd found on top of the dresser. On its cover was the photograph of a single terracotta warrior. The soldier's attire was more lavish than most of the warriors I'd seen. Its clay armor looked like rich leather, with stitched plating and knots of ribbon tied at the joints. Red and blue paint, flaking and faded, was still visible on its armor and face.

Zac handed the brochure to Jason. "Why does he look so different than the rest of them?"

"A terracotta warrior's armor was based on rank," said Jason, thumbing through the brochure. "The more decorated officers, like lieutenants and whatnot, wore more extravagant gear."

"Could he be the Shoemaker?" I asked.

"Hmmm, I don't think so."

"Why not?"

He showed me the brochure's cover. Above the warrior's picture was a caption of text reading: WHO WAS GENERAL LI FEI?

"I don't believe a general would've been a shoemaker," he said. "Those jobs were for peasants. Leaders of armies tended to be of noble birth."

"Then who is he?"

Jason opened the brochure. He read aloud:

WHO WAS GENERAL LI FEI?

When Americans think of historical betrayals, they often remember Benedict Arnold—an American general during the American Revolution who famously defected to the British army. But when the Chinese remember traitorous acts, they recall Li Fei—a general during the Warring States Period who famously betrayed the First Qin Emperor of China.

Yet before committing treason, General Li was Emperor Qin's most trusted friend. Together they conquered all of China, uniting the barbaric Warring States under one powerful ruler through sheer military might. They standardized China's currency, built canals, roads, and began construction of the Great Wall making China more prosperous than ever before.

However, thousands of workers died on these public works projects. Emperor Qin even ordered the killings of scholars who opposed his ideas, and he approved the executions of workers who built his tomb to keep its location and treasures secret.

"Wait, slow down," I said. "This is too much like history class and you're losing me. Can you simplify this story in, like, Maddie-speak?"

"Maddie-speak?"

"Yeah, you know, in terms I can follow."

"Okay . . ." Jason rolled his eyes. "Well, this General Li guy didn't like what Emperor Qin had done to the scholars because he was, like, a follower of their teachings."

"The emperor killed his teachers. Gotcha."

"So General Li threatened to kill the emperor."

"And that's bad, right?"

"Of course it's bad," Jason said. "Emperor Qin was viewed as a god. When General Li brandished his sword, he sentenced himself to death. But when it came time for Li's execution, Emperor Qin couldn't bring himself to kill his friend. So he exiled the general instead."

"To where?"

"It says here . . ." Jason skimmed through the brochure's text. "The general fled to China's outskirts near a place where the Great Wall was being built. Anyway, more scholars and workers were slain. General Li's anger grew. He began raising an army to overthrow Emperor Qin."

"Oooh, this sounds a lot like Game of Thrones."

"Sort of," Jason said. "But in the end, it didn't work out for General Li."

"Why not?"

"Well, after years of training his army he returned to defeat the emperor, but he only had about 6,000 warriors—whereas Emperor Qin had tens of thousands. General Li couldn't win with his inferior numbers. He was defeated in battle. And this time, Emperor Qin wasn't playing around because he ordered not only the general's execution, but his surviving army too."

"Ouch," I said.

"Yeah, the poor guy had to watch as his men were killed."

"Okay, that sucks—but something doesn't make sense."

"What?"

"If General Li was a traitor, why would there be a terracotta statue of him at Emperor Qin's burial site?"

"Well, it seems Emperor Qin still wanted to honor his friend despite their falling out," Jason said. "So he commissioned a statue of General Li to stand guard over his tomb."

"Wow," Zac finally spoke. "Talk about a twisted friendship."

"For real," Jason said.

"It's a pretty cool story," I admitted. "We should check out the general's statue when we visit the museum—"

BOOM.

The front door rattled. I sat bolt upright, staring at the door. Someone was outside, knocking to come in.

Chapter 31

BOOM.

They knocked again. Zac flinched. We glanced at each other wondering who it could be. Tamora had said she would arrive in twenty-four hours, so it couldn't be her. What if it was Rico and his goons? Or gangsters of the Chinese Triad? Assassins? I scooted off the bed and tip-toed to the door.

"Maddie," whispered Jason. "What are you doing?"

BOOM. Geez, why'd they have to knock so forcefully?

"Who's there?" I shouted. "I warn you—I'm armed!"

There was a pause. Then—

"Room service."

I breathed a sigh of relief and opened the door. An attendant stood in the hall wearing a white apron and hat with a serving table of food. On top of the cart, fancy silver-domed lids covered our meals. The attendant wheeled the serving table inside, bowed, and returned to the hall. I shut the door behind him.

"You—are—nuts—Maddie," said Jason. "That could've been a bad guy."

I shrugged. "What can I say? I'm starving."

We attacked the food. I was so hungry I don't think I tasted a single bite until I slowed down to enjoy the dragon's beard candy, which reminded me of cotton candy, though not as sweet. Afterward, I crawled into bed and was fast asleep in seconds.

The next day, I woke up early and ordered breakfast. The television included American stations, and I turned on CNN hoping they'd air another story about Rico. The news anchor's serious voice droned on in the background as I got dressed.

"And you won't believe this," the news anchor said. *"A fourteen-year-old girl in Evansville, Indiana has kidnapped her father. Maddie Jones and her two younger brothers are suspects in their dad's disappearance."*

I dropped my Converse high-tops and stared at the TV.

"The Jones children are still missing after they mysteriously escaped from the Evansville State Hospital. Maddie Jones was hospitalized following a car accident last Tuesday on Highway 62. The car had flipped and skidded for several hundred feet before exploding. Two victims were found dead at the scene.

"Initially, authorities did not suspect Maddie of kidnapping her father—until security footage from her dad's museum showed her breaking and entering and vandalizing his office."

Grainy black and white video of me smashing the museum's glass door played onscreen.

"If you see Maddie Jones, do not approach. She is considered armed and dangerous. Some of the crimes she has committed include posing as a cop and redirecting traffic, to replacing an entire Krispy Kreme's donut filling with mayonnaise—which means Maddie may be

mentally unstable. Police urge anyone with information to contact the following crime-stoppers hotline."

A phone number appeared onscreen along with pictures of me and my brothers. The photos had been taken from our school's yearbook.

Why'd they have to use that horrible picture? I thought.

"Look, we're famous," said Zac.

"I believe you mean infamous," Jason corrected.

"Same thing."

"Not even close."

I groaned.

"What's wrong?" asked Zac.

"Look at that picture!" I said, exasperated. "My hair is all over the place and I'm not even wearing make-up. Ugh, I'll never forget which day is picture day again, I can promise you that."

"Erm," said Jason. "I think you should reconsider your priorities."

"Shut up!"

Twenty minutes later, after shoveling bacon and eggs into my mouth, I threw on my compass necklace and stormed out of the hotel room. There was only one way to clear our names now . . . saving Dad.

Chapter 32

WITH HELP FROM THE CONCIERGE, we were able to purchase transportation cards, which we learned were needed to ride buses around town. The concierge informed us that the nearest bus stop was five blocks away, and we exited the hotel feeling confident we'd learn more about the Shoemaker at the Museum of Terracotta Warriors. A crisp autumn breeze drifted off the sidewalk, and brought with it rustling leaves and the scent of freshly paved asphalt.

"Hey, where are you kids going?" I turned to see Mr. Yao, the limousine driver, waiting outside and leaning against his car. "Tàitài Rose gave specific instructions," he yelled across the parking lot. "And she told me you stay inside, no come out."

He started walking in our direction.

"Well, crap," said Zac. "What'd we do now?"

"Isn't it obvious," I said. *"Run!"*

We sprinted away from Mr. Yao and ran across the parking lot, turned down a street and bolted into an alleyway.

But Mr. Yao chased us. Despite his age, he kept up fairly well, because two blocks later I stole a glance over my shoulder and saw him running thirty yards behind. We emerged from the alleyway.

"Which way?" shouted Jason.

"Erm, over there!" I shouted, trying to remember the concierge's directions.

We ran across the street, dodging traffic, and bolted down another dark alleyway sandwiched between two buildings with yellow and blue facades. The alleyway was littered with overflowing dumpsters and feral cats. The animals skittered away to hide as we darted past.

Jason glanced back to find Mr. Yao. "This—dude—can—run," he panted.

I looked over my shoulder. Mr. Yao was closer than before. Dang, this old guy needed to start a workout channel on YouTube.

We exited the alleyway, and I broke left and cut across a grassy field. Ahead of us, I saw a bus rolling through a stop sign and turning a corner. It stopped at a covered bench where passengers were waiting.

"We're about to miss our ride," yelled Jason.

"Faster," I shouted, and Zac suddenly went sprinting past. Holy cow, he was fast. No wonder he played, like, all the sports.

We reached the bus as it was pulling away. I ran up beside its entry door and banged on the glass.

But the bus kept going. Its driver didn't see me.

I banged again. *Stop, let us on!*

The driver glanced over at the noise, and saw me. He slammed on the brakes and the bus screeched to a stop. The doors opened, and the driver shouted something at me in Mandarin. I'm pretty sure he was cussing.

We boarded the bus and swiped our transportation cards. The boys sat in the vacant seat right behind the driver, but I didn't sit. Instead, I stood near the entrance and glanced outside to find Mr. Yao.

There he was, running the last leg across the grassy field. He waved his arms in the air signaling the bus to wait.

"Let's go," I told the driver.

But he didn't understand me since I spoke English, and now all of a sudden he didn't appear to be in a hurry. Mr. Yao crossed the street, rounded the bus, and sprinted up its side. He was almost to the open door.

"GO!"

I pulled the mechanism and shut the door. Then I stepped on the driver's foot, gunning the gas. The bus lurched forward. Passengers screamed. I grabbed the steering wheel and steered the bus left to avoid a parked car. The driver slapped at my hand, yelling in Mandarin. I couldn't understand him, but it was apparent—the driver was ticked!

Go figure. It's not every day a fourteen-year-old girl takes over your bus route.

I let go of the wheel and backed away. The driver pointed at a seat and shouted again. I sat where he motioned, and he turned his attention to the road mumbling words beneath his breath. I glanced out the window to find Mr. Yao. The poor guy was doubled over panting for air.

"Tamora is going to be really mad now," said Jason.

"From this point forward," I said, bringing my attention back inside the bus. "Consider ourselves grounded for the next several years."

Chapter 33

THE BUS STOPPED OUTSIDE THE Museum of Terracotta Warriors. We exited (the driver glaring at me like he wanted to wring my neck) and several tourists joined us. Among them were an American family, a French couple, and a group of Japanese people with cameras hanging around their necks. A winding path led to the museum's entrance.

The place was impressive.

Colorful orange and black banners with images of terracotta warriors fluttered in the wind. The museum itself was a beautifully constructed mansion, its Chinese architecture symmetrical with its roof flaring out at the corners. Surrounding the building were lush gardens, and behind it, a huge earthen mound loomed in the distance the size of a small mountain.

Jason pointed at the building. "Technically, that's not the museum. The entire exhibit stretches several miles around the mound. They've found terracotta warriors all over the property."

We walked the winding path, enjoying the view and fresh scents of daffodils and orchids from the gardens. It was hard to believe this place was built to be the grave for one man.

I watched as the American family stopped to take pictures, posing with a selfie stick. They were all smiling and laughing and filled with excitement. Their joy reminded me of a vacation we had taken with Dad to visit the Cahokia Indian mounds in Illinois last year. It had been a fun day. After climbing to the top of the largest earthen pyramid north of Mesoamerica, we took a family photo.

Seeing the family reminded me how dangerous our situation was. Mom was already gone. If we lost Dad . . .

I cleared my throat. "When did the brochure say tours began?"

"In just a few minutes," said Jason.

We went inside and purchased tickets.

A small Chinese woman led the museum tour.

She walked up front, guiding us through the enclosed hangar constructed around the discovery site, past long columns of clay warriors standing in precise military formation. The warriors' tunics, armored vests, goatees, mustaches, and close-cropped beards were all so different. Not one statue looked the same as another, like a throng of strangers you'd meet on the streets of Shanghai.

It blew my mind these statues were 2,000 years old.

She gathered us around a ten-foot-long bronze chariot drawn by four bronze horses, and told us how the site had an estimated 6,000 warriors and some 500 horses, all organized to protect the Tomb of the First Qin Emperor. She pointed our attention to the chariot's design and its intricate carvings. I tried to listen to what she had to say because it was the kind of stuff my dad would've loved, but my brothers had started talking about the emperor's tomb.

"I bet it's deep beneath the mound," said Zac.

"It is," Jason assured. "But it's never been excavated because the Chinese government is afraid of destroying the artifacts inside. They're waiting until new technology is available before beginning a dig."

I pulled out Dad's map. "Are we in Pit One?"

"Yes, there are 6,000 warriors in this pit alone."

I read over Dad's notes: *There are eleven corridors, but seek the seventh. Seven rows back, middle soldier.*

I glanced up at the columns of warriors. The clay soldiers were entrenched in long corridors separated by low earthen walls. As I scanned left to right, I counted eleven corridors.

Bingo.

The tour guide pressed on, leading our group to an adjacent room. Now was our chance. We hung back and waited for everyone to pass. And on the count of three, we slipped over the railing to sneak behind the first row of terracotta warriors . . .

Chapter 34

"EXCUSE ME, YOU'RE NOT ALLOWED to go back there," the tour guide said.

Fetch. She'd caught us. We eased back over the railing, my cheeks flushed at being spotted so easily. No longer able to sneak away, we continued on with the tour.

We were led to a room with a single terracotta warrior on display. The statue's clay armor was elaborate, its leather plating stitched with a ribbon tied at the joints. The warrior's eyes were listless, and a mustache curled flamboyantly above his lips. A plaque beneath the soldier read: GENERAL LI FEI.

The tour guide began telling us about the general's tumultuous past and how he died at the hands of his friend, the emperor. It was an interesting story, but we'd learned it already from the hotel brochure.

Zac nudged me in the ribs. "How are we going to break away from the group?"

"I'm thinking," I whispered.

But no ideas sprung to mind. We followed the tour into the next room, this one devoted to Emperor Qin. Another chariot and horses were behind a roped-off area. This chariot was different than the one we saw earlier—it was enclosed so the rider could be hidden from the public's curious eyes. Along the walls, paintings of the emperor and Old China depicted different events from his life.

"The First Qin Emperor," the tour guide said, "built his tomb to be an underground palace, one that would allow him to conquer death. He was obsessed with immortality. His burial chamber, which has never been opened, is said to be filled with a treasury of riches—piles of precious gemstones representing the stars, sun, and moon."

I grunted, realizing something.

"What is it?" asked Jason.

"That must be what Rico is after," I said. "Emperor Qin's untouched riches."

"Now if you will all follow me this way," the tour guide said.

She moved the group along, but I had a sudden idea. I waited until the tour had fully disappeared from the room, then I slipped beneath the ropes surrounding the chariot and horses.

"Maddie, what are you doing?"

I pried open the chariot's doors. "Quick, get inside." My brothers looked at me with wide eyes, but they bent beneath the ropes and we all clambered inside of the chariot. I shut the door behind us.

It was cramped. The air tasted stale. Stray light filtered between cracks. Dust floated in the rays. I held my breath and listened. It sounded like the tour guide had returned, her shoes scuffing against the floor. Through a crack in the chariot, I saw her stop and look around, but she didn't seem to realize where we were. She turned and rejoined the group.

Yes!

"Now what?" breathed Zac.

"We wait," I whispered. "And once the museum closes, we'll sneak out and inspect the seventh corridor for the seventh-row soldier."

Chapter 35

HOURS PASSED. THE TEMPERATURE ROSE. It grew clammy and hot. I wiped sweat from my brow and took off my jacket, but the stagnant air was stifling and I couldn't get comfortable. Tour guides continued leading groups, and every so often someone would approach to admire the chariot and horses. Each time they approached, we held our breaths and listened as they discussed the chariot's beautiful artistry.

Around lunchtime, things got worse.

The boys and I were lying side by side like we slept in a small tent, and Zac had to pee. He didn't think he could hold it, and we threatened him with a painful death if we felt anything wet pooling beneath us. Jason opened his backpack, offering us each a banana and peanut butter crackers (explaining he'd confiscated them from the hotel lobby earlier that morning). It wasn't a four-course meal, but the meager lunch was better than nothing.

Eventually, boredom sank in and I fell asleep.

I dreamed about the Shoemaker. He was a clay statue trying to speak, but I couldn't understand him because his lips were stitched closed. His message seemed important, like it could save my life or my family's, but no matter how hard I strained to listen his words came out mumbled.

A shadowy figure appeared, looming ominously over me with a huge curved sword. The Shadow cackled, his laugh giving me goosebumps, and I knew deep down that if I'd heard the Shoemaker's message I might've survived the coming attack. The Shadow raised its sword, and as the blade came swinging down I screamed—

Jason nudged me awake.

"It's time," he whispered.

I rubbed my eyes. There was no Shadow. No sword or Shoemaker. I glanced through the chariot's cracks and saw that the lighting in Emperor Qin's exhibit room had been dimmed. It was quiet. The typical chatter we'd heard throughout the day had ceased.

"What time is it?" I croaked, still half-asleep.

"Half past seven. The place closed thirty minutes ago."

Goodness, we'd been hiding for nearly ten hours. My body ached. I grabbed my jacket, which I'd been using as a pillow, and exited the chariot. As I got out and stretched, Zac bumped into me and stormed toward a door labeled BATHROOM. He crashed into it, fumbled for the handle, and rushed inside. On second thought, a potty break sounded like a pretty good idea. After doing our business, and drinking lukewarm water from a fountain, the three of us entered Pit One together.

Ghostly light from exit signs provided just enough illumination to navigate. In relative darkness, the terracotta warriors looked almost lifelike. The place now felt eerie, and I couldn't help but think the clay soldiers would spring to life any moment, impaling us with their swords, spears, and axes. I mean, come on, these guys had guarded Emperor

Qin's tomb for 2,000 years. Now my brothers and I had arrived with Dad's map—a clue to unlock ancient secrets. I should've been excited, but I got a feeling that whatever we were about to find might be dreadful.

We hopped a railing separating museum visitors from the terracotta warriors. I landed on compact dirt—the same ground these soldiers stood on when they were first placed here. When I stood tall, I came face to face with a warrior. His blank eyes stared tirelessly forward, a determined look on his sculpted face, and he was as tall as me.

Creepy.

"Let's find the Shoemaker," said Jason.

We crept through the throng of tightly packed warriors. There were so many of them that sometimes it was hard to squeeze past. Finally, we reached the seventh corridor.

Right smack in the middle, I thought. I was willing to bet the soldier we sought would be at the heart of this row.

"Remember," Jason crept forward, and Zac and I followed, "the terracotta warriors were given stamps—signatures—but one is unique . . ."

"Yeah, yeah, the Shoemaker," I said. "Let's just find him and get out of here."

A strange sensation came over me as we moved between the clay soldiers, a feeling of being watched. Shadows seemed to stir. And if my eyes weren't deceiving me, it appeared the terracotta warriors' heads turned ever so slightly to stare as we passed.

But when I snapped my gaze around, the warriors were all facing forward. Their heads hadn't moved.

"Is that him?" asked Zac, pointing.

He pointed at the warrior in the middle of the seventh row. The warrior looked no different than the others. His tunic and armored vest were nearly identical to the others, but his cropped beard and facial features were certainly unique. Every warrior's face looked like a different person. What was so special about this warrior?

We stood on three sides of him, looking him up and down. "What are we looking for, exactly?" I asked, peering into the Shoemaker's listless eyes. I shuddered upon remembering my dream.

"The signature," said Jason.

"Yeah, I know that, but what will it look like?"

"It will be a Chinese letter," he said. "Each warrior was stamped with the signature of whoever made him. That way if there were flaws, Emperor Qin would know who to punish."

"Geez," Zac whistled.

Jason shrugged. "Qin was ruthless."

"Well, I don't see anything," I said. "Do either of you?"

Jason ran his hands along the warrior's armor, arms, and legs to feel for . . . whatever it was we were supposed to find. He turned on his phone's flashlight and shined it on the soldier, but he didn't appear to find anything.

"Er—the stamp should be right here."

He pointed our attention to the warrior's right shoulder, then swept his light to an adjacent warrior, showing us its stamp. Sure enough, every warrior we glanced at had a Chinese letter stamped in the same location.

All except the Shoemaker.

"What does Dad's map say?" asked Zac.

I pulled it from my pocket and unfolded its fine parchment. Jason shined his phone's light so we could see it, but reading over Dad's notes didn't tell us anything different. A hand-drawn image of a single terracotta warrior was to the right of the map's labyrinthine passageways. And something else. Something I hadn't noticed before.

The warrior's shoe had been circled.

We looked at each other and smiled. The three of us dropped to our hands and knees, searching around the warrior's shoes. I brushed away dirt so I could get a better look at the warrior's heel . . . and I found the stamp. A Chinese letter. I rubbed my thumb across it, and the stamp pressed in like a button. On the other shoe, a compartment popped open.

And a yellowed scroll tumbled out.

Chapter 36

THE SCROLL WAS ANCIENT, POSSIBLY older than Dad's map. Thin and brittle, it was no wider than my hand when I unrolled it.

"What's it say?" asked Jason, and I could hear a twinge of excitement in his voice.

There were markings all over the scroll, but none of it legible. "I can't read it," I said. "It's written in Chinese."

BANG!

The noise startled us. It came from somewhere overhead. I glanced up, and saw a blade of fire appear in the ceiling, cutting a circle in the roof big enough for a man to fit inside. It sounded like a blowtorch. A neatly-cut ceiling tile came crashing to the ground. Then more flames appeared as blowtorches were used to cut holes all over the ceiling. Tiles came crashing down with loud bangs. Ropes tumbled down the holes to the floor.

Soldiers appeared. They repelled down the ropes into the museum. They wore all black and Kevlar vests. Assault rifles were strapped to their shoulders and night vision goggles covered their faces. Oh, fetch! These guys were armed for war.

We were screwed.

"It's Rico's goons," I mouthed to my brothers. "Quick, hide!"

We crawled on our hands and knees between ancient warriors just as the modern-day soldiers hit the ground along the perimeter of the museum. As soon as their boots touched down, they dashed left or right with their guns shouldered. It looked like they searched the area for threats like tactical SWAT teams do in movies. We watched from our hidden position, and my mind raced for ways to escape.

There's the entrance near the front, I thought. *And the exit near Emperor Qin's exhibit room.*

But both routes were quickly being cut off by soldiers as they set up guards at each corner and along the walls. The guards faced the terracotta warriors, night vision goggles searching, guns aimed and deadly.

Gulp.

A giant of a man walked into view. Bald. Dark skin. He was outfitted in full military gear with two large pistols tucked inside shoulder holsters. Although he wasn't wearing an Armani suit like I'd seen in Detective Murphy's photographs, or the news video when boarding the plane, I recognized him as Rico Raja at once. He wore wired earbuds that were connected to a device in his hand. An iPod? Cell phone? I wasn't sure. He seemed to be mumbling to himself, talking into the device or something. Was he recording his voice?

"The men are in position, sir." A slender man with black hair tucked behind his ears walked into view and stood beside Rico. His build was smaller, shorter, and more agile looking. I shivered. It was the man with the tattooed hand.

Rico pocketed the device and removed his earbuds. "Bring me the doctor," he said with a strong accent that might've been Middle-Eastern.

Jason edged closer. "Maddie," he whispered. "What'd we do?"

I had no idea. Jason and Zac looked up to me during times like this. I was the one who typically kept my cool when trouble came to catch us. But I'd never faced a situation this dire. How could I tell Jason I was secretly flipping out and still sound like I had my crap together?

Truth was, I couldn't.

And he would know if I lied.

So I cleared my throat and prepared to tell him our number was up . . .

. . . when a bedraggled-looking man with a scraggly beard was shoved roughly to his knees in front of Rico. His plaid shirt was torn and half-tucked, khaki pants dirtied, and his vintage-framed glasses were crooked on his nose.

My heart did a somersault.

Jason and Zac gasped.

It was Dad. In horrible shape—I'd never seen him looking so rough.

"Dr. Jones," said Rico, his oily voice prickling my skin as though the devil himself had spoken. "Your expertise has proven most useful. This place," he swept his arm out at the army of terracotta warriors, "is magnificent, no?"

Dad sniffled as he stared at the ground.

"Your work for the Chinese government—what did you discover? If ever you were to speak, now would be the time."

Dad remained quiet.

"You disappoint me, Dr. Jones." Rico knelt so he met face-to-face with my father. "I thought you might be more cooperative once we arrived. Alas, it appears I must force your hand. It's time I shared a secret . . .

"I kidnapped your children."

Liar! I thought.

But Dad didn't know that. He struggled to break free, cursing and spitting, but the man with the tattooed hand kept him constrained.

"Yes, yes, I knew that would get your attention." Rico clenched his massive fists as he stared at my father. "The children are unharmed, I promise you, but torture can be arranged if you continue to resist."

"You keep your grubby hands off them!" Dad shouted.

The man with the tattooed hand hit him in the back of the head with the butt of a pistol. Dad collapsed to the ground. Zac started to rise, but I grabbed his wrist and held him tight. "No," I breathed.

Zac's look was murder.

"You have trained them well," Rico went on. "They lie to my face, claiming to know nothing of the map."

"That's because they don't," Dad croaked.

"Hmm, I'm not so sure. Perhaps if you tell me the map's secrets, I won't need to harm your children."

"You—you leave them alone!"

"That depends entirely on you, Dr. Jones." Rico grabbed one of his holstered pistols and cocked it. "I'm going to present you with two choices. Tell me the map's secrets. Or I'll torture your children and then you can tell me."

Dad screamed and head-butted Rico.

Rico shouted in pain and sprang back, clutching his face. Blood streamed through his fingers and the veins in his neck were bulging. "You've broken my nose," he snarled. "You shouldn't have done that, Dr. Jones."

He shoved the pistol into Dad's temple, and pulled the trigger.

Chapter 37

CLICK. THE GUN DIDN'T FIRE. Its chamber must've been empty.

Rico laughed. "Did you think I was finished with you, Dr. Jones?"

Dad scoffed, but his tone sounded shaky. Rico pulling that trigger had clearly unnerved him.

Rico clutched his broken nose and snapped it back into place. "*Argh*—you are a difficult man to crack, Dr. Jones. Threatening your life appears to be a waste of time. But perhaps torturing your daughter will change your mind—" he motioned to the man with the tattooed hand. "Zheng, retrieve the girl."

Zheng clenched his tattooed hand and marched away.

"*NO!*" my father shouted.

"Hold," said Rico, and Zheng stopped in his tracks. "Are you finally willing to cooperate, Dr. Jones?"

Dad hesitated, but I saw a quick nod of his head.

"Then how do we open Emperor Qin's tomb?"

Dad climbed unsteadily to his feet. "There's a terracotta warrior in this museum," he said, adjusting his glasses, "who has a clue hidden inside of his boot."

"Which warrior?"

Dad mumbled something I couldn't quite hear.

Rico snapped his fingers, and Zheng started to depart.

"Wait, all right." Dad pointed in our direction. "Seventh corridor. Seventh row, middle soldier."

Oh, fetch! Dad unknowingly pointed right at us.

Rico smiled, holstering his pistol. "Lynch," he called.

A new figure emerged—the scarred goon whose eye I had jabbed back in Evansville. He now wore an eyepatch, and although I knew he earned the facial accessory because of me, his tactical gear and assault rifle were no joking matter.

"Search for this warrior," Rico commanded.

Lynch shouldered his weapon and moved to obey. He hopped the railing and dropped to the dirt floor the terracotta warriors stood on. From behind, I heard more soldiers' boots stomping into the pit. Lynch wasn't the only mercenary fast approaching our location. Holy frigging crap! The soldiers were about to surround us.

"Move, move," I told the boys, and we crept as quickly—and as quietly—as we could to the end of our corridor. We slipped into the next corridor, number eight I believe, just as mercenaries arrived at number seven. They marched past us, their faces pressing forward and not looking in our direction. They headed for the Shoemaker.

We crept deeper into the ranks of terracotta warriors within our row, hoping the ancient soldiers gave us enough cover to stay hidden. My heart was racing. Sweat beaded on my brow. Dirt brushed through my fingers as I crawled on my hands and knees.

"I found it," Lynch suddenly shouted. "But it looks like somebody has already been here?"

"What? How?" Rico yelled back.

"A hidden compartment has been opened," Lynch explained. "And its contents are missing."

Rico's yell of rage echoed throughout the museum, sending a chill down my spine.

"Wait," shouted Lynch. "There are sneaker tracks in the dirt. Whoever looted the soldier is still here!"

Chapter 38

MERCENARIES PATROLLED PIT ONE, searching each corridor and along the perimeter of the museum. For nearly ten minutes the boys and I crawled on our hands and knees, weaving in and out of terracotta warriors, dodging their every move. But I knew we couldn't avoid these guys much longer. There were just too many of them. Plus, we couldn't hide the tracks we'd made in the dirt.

We reached an area overlooking Emperor Qin's exhibit room—and the chariot we'd hidden inside earlier in the day. An exit sign loomed beyond the room. It looked as though we had two options: hide inside the chariot again or sneak outside through the exit.

But a mercenary swept past, night vision goggles searching. We crouched behind warriors so he wouldn't spot us. I held my breath as he passed. The soldier turned down an adjacent corridor, disappearing from view. Oh, fetch that was close!

"On the count of three," I whispered. "Run for the chariot."

Jason nodded. Zac gave me a thumbs-up.

"One. Two. Thr—"

Jason's phone suddenly *dinged* with a text, loud and alerting. Jason snatched his phone from his pocket and silenced it. "Sorry," he apologized. His eyes widened upon seeing the message. "It's Tamora. Her plane just landed in China."

"And our troubles worsen," I mumbled.

"The noise came from over there!"

Boots thudded heavily as mercenaries closed in on our position. We had to act now or we'd lose our only escape.

"Go!" I said.

Zac bounded into the open first, climbed the railing, and darted for the chariot. Jason and I raced after him. I didn't look back. My legs felt sluggish, but pure adrenaline sped me forward. We were almost to the chariot when—

—Zac was grabbed by Zheng, the man with the tattooed hand.

Jason and I skidded to a stop.

"Don't hurt him!" I yelled.

Zheng cackled, his tattooed hand clenched around Zac's neck. "But that would spoil the fun," he said, his accent imbued with a hint of Mandarin.

"I swear if you harm him—"

"You'll what? Tell your daddy?"

That's it, I thought, taking a step forward. *This guy deserves a good kick in the—*

Strong hands grabbed me from behind, lifting me from the ground. A second mercenary seized Jason. He kicked and fought to get away. I squirmed and twisted, but whoever had me was simply too strong.

"Thought you'd seen the last of me?" growled my captor, his breath stinking of rotten eggs. A glance told me it was Lynch, the goon with the eyepatch.

"Ugh," I groaned. "You seriously need a breath mint, dude."

Chapter 39

WE WERE BROUGHT BEFORE RICO. He was surrounded by mercenaries. One of the soldiers must have removed the Shoemaker's hidden compartment drawer because Rico was inspecting it as we approached.

"We flushed out the rats," growled Lynch. He shoved me roughly forward, right into my father. Dad caught me in his arms, a puzzled expression across his face.

"Maddie . . . ?"

"Hi, Dad."

"But how—"

"It's a long story, Dad."

"Ah, the children," said Rico, handing the tiny drawer back to a mercenary. "And to think, for a moment I believed Dr. Jones when he said his children knew nothing of the map."

"They don't," my dad said.

"And yet here they are." Rico looked directly at me. "Give me the clue you discovered."

The Shoemaker's scroll was in my pocket. But I couldn't give it to Rico. If he could somehow translate its ancient script, then he'd likely get access to Emperor Qin's tomb. And according to Dad's notes that could be dangerous—I didn't know why. Besides, the last thing the world needed was one more rich man stealing what didn't belong to him. I inhaled a deep breath, putting confidence in my voice.

"We didn't find anything."

Rico clenched his jaw, his scowl hard and deadly. "Do you take me for a fool, girl?"

"Well . . ." I said slowly.

"*Silence!*"

I flinched.

He grabbed a pistol from his shoulder holster—and this time, he loaded it right before my eyes. "I have a daughter of my own," he said as he cocked the gun's hammer, putting a bullet into the chamber. "About your age. She is pretty, not unlike yourself. I will do anything for her. *Anything*," he emphasized the word.

"That's cool," I tried to sound nonchalant, but the loaded gun made me nervous.

"Being a father, I find it difficult to harm a child," he placed the gun against my dad's head. "But I have no issues killing an adult to achieve my goals. And this time, I *will* shoot your father. Where is the clue?"

"No—" my dad's voice broke. "Not in front of my children."

"That's not up to you, Dr. Jones. It's up to . . ." he looked at me as if wanting my name.

"M-Maddie," my voice quivered.

"Maddie," he grunted. "Your father's life is now in your hands. Five seconds."

Jason wriggled to break free from the mercenary restraining him—but with no luck. "Don't do it, Maddie. He's bluffing!"

"Four."

Zac, still held captive by Zheng with the tattooed hand, had tears blurring his eyes. "Dad," he cried.

"Three."

I glanced at Dad. His eyes were pleading, almost trying to tell me something. I wasn't sure what.

"Two."

"All right—here—take it!" I reached into my pocket and revealed the aging parchment.

Rico snatched it from my hand, the ghost of a smile spreading across his lips as he unrolled the scroll. "The next clue," he breathed. "Chinese. Possibly a dialect of the Qin Dynasty. Zheng, can you read it?"

He handed the scroll to Zheng, who let go of Zac to read over the parchment.

"You are a clever man, Dr. Jones." Rico holstered his pistol. "It's a shame you wouldn't accept my offer when I visited your museum last week."

"I believe in the restoration of historical relics," Dad said. "They shouldn't be tampered with by amateurs or stolen by private collectors."

"I care not for Qin's relics."

"Then why are you here?"

"Zheng—can you decipher the scroll?"

"Yes," said Zheng. "It's a Wǔshén spell—old magic— exactly what we've been searching for." His face twisted into a smile, eyes gleaming with crazed enthusiasm. "And with this spell, we can open Emperor Qin's tomb."

Chapter 40

SPELLS. OLD MAGIC. WHAT THE heck did these madmen have for lunch? A burrito that makes you hallucinate? I was about to tell them they were all a bunch of whackos who needed to visit an insane asylum, when my dad did something totally unexpected.

He jabbed Lynch in his good eye.

"Arrgggh!" Lynch screamed as he clutched his wounded face, letting go of me.

Everyone's focus turned to the distraction. Zac and I made eye contact, and we both seemed to realize we were free from our captors—since Zheng had let go of him to read the Shoemaker's scroll. Zac turned toward the mercenary holding Jason, and he kicked him right in the junk. The mercenary doubled over, grabbing his groin.

"*RUN!*" Dad shouted.

We bolted to get away.

Guns must have been drawn and aimed because Rico yelled: "No shooting! I need the doctor alive! Go after them!"

And a chase ensued.

The mercenaries ran after us. I raced beside Dad and my brothers through Pit One, into Emperor Qin's exhibit room, and out the exit. Outside, the moon was bright, but clouds scudding across it kept throwing us into darkness. A heavy fog lay on the ground. Ahead, I could see a wooded area beyond an outlying building with lighted windows. Then I heard someone shout.

"Fetching hell, where'd they go?"

My heart rose. If we could just get to those trees we might be able to escape.

"Maddie—" my dad panted beside me. "We won't make it."

"What? Why?" I breathed.

"If I go with you—" we reached the copse of trees. The boys crashed through the brush and kept running, but Dad stopped. "—then Rico will open Emperor Qin's tomb and all may be doomed."

"Dad, that's crazy talk—let's go!"

"The tomb is a prison keeping great evil locked away. I thought Rico was after Qin's treasures, but now I'm not so sure. There's something else at stake here, and I must stay behind to delay his plans."

"But Dad—"

"Rico needs me to decipher clues. I can mislead him, keep him from getting to Qin's sarcophagus."

"I can't let you do this. If Rico gets what he wants— he'll kill you!"

Dad smiled, though it didn't touch the corners of his eyes. "You are so much like your mother."

In the distance, mercenary flashlights sparked into view. I was pretty sure some of them would be armed with night vision goggles—they'd spot us any moment.

"One last thing, Maddie. If the tomb is opened . . . search my Cloud account." He must've seen my puzzled expression, because he added, "Do you remember our vacation to Mexico City when we visited Teotihuacán?"

I nodded.

"Search through our vacation photos—"

Men shouting told me the mercenaries had spotted us.

"Because if the tomb is opened, you may be our only hope. Now go!" He kissed my forehead and urged me to run.

And I, fearful for my dad, not wanting to leave his side after all we'd done to try and save him, ran through the dark forest while mercenaries wrestled him to the ground.

Chapter 41

I WAS RUNNING AND REALIZED that I no longer knew exactly what I was doing, or where I was. Somehow my instincts brought me back to the woods outside the Museum of Terracotta Warriors, where I sprinted blindly through the trees. A root caught my ankle and I tripped, stumbling to my knees. A sharp pain lanced through my ankle.

I cried out in pain and tried to roll my ankle, but it hurt too much to wriggle it around. The earthen ground felt damp and the smell of moss permeated the air. I pushed myself up on my hands to peer back the way I came, trying to see if mercenaries followed in pursuit, but the woods were too dark. The moonlight was shrouded by a dense forest canopy. Faintly, I heard the sounds of struggle on the edge of the forest as mercenaries captured my father. Arguing broke out.

". . . go after the children."

"Leave them. We've got the archaeologist."

"But Rico said—"

"—to capture the doctor. And we did. Now let's rendezvous with the others."

My chest ached. We'd rescued Dad and fled the scene, only for him to not come with us. He had entrusted me with a new task, but I was afraid. What if Dad's life ended tonight because I couldn't find the courage to keep going? What if I wasn't smart enough to decipher his cryptic words about our vacation to Mexico?

The hell with that, I thought. *Get up, Maddie Jones. Fight the fear and save your father!*

I climbed to my feet, hardly able to stand on my throbbing ankle. I listened for several moments before I thought it was safe to leave. When all I heard were the hoots of owls and the skittering of animals in the brush, I finally got moving. With my sprained ankle, the best I could do was limp along at a moderate pace.

Where are the boys? I thought, peering around the forest.

I hobbled through the woods using the trees to support my weight. After several minutes of navigating the dark forest alone, I heard my name being called.

"Maddie, over here!"

I limped toward the voice, and found my brothers hiding behind a copse of trees on the outskirts of the woods. I knelt beside them. A lonely road snaked its way beside the forest, disappearing around a bend.

"Where's Dad?" asked Zac, concern in his voice.

I told them what happened after getting separated—how Dad stayed behind to thwart Rico's plans, the mercenaries catching him, spraining my ankle, and how the mercenaries left to meet up with the rest of their group.

"Do you think they followed you?" asked Jason.

"I don't think so," I said.

"Now what'd we do?" asked Zac.

"Isn't it obvious?" said Jason. "We gotta save Dad."

"But how?" Zac protested. "They're grown-ups and they have guns."

I recalled Dad's parting words of wisdom. "We need a place with Wi-Fi."

"Oh, yeah, because internet access will help save our father."

"No, hear me out." And I explained how Dad told me to access his Cloud account if things got dicey.

Jason shook his head. "We don't need Wi-Fi, I've got a phone." But when he powered it on, he swore. "Fetch. No service."

"So Wi-Fi it is."

"Yeah, but where?" Zac motioned to our surroundings. "We're beside a road in the middle of nowhere."

"Roads lead to places," I pointed out.

"But this one might stretch for miles and miles."

"It won't," I promised, and I reminded them that Xi'an was one of China's biggest cities. The Museum of Terracotta Warriors was nestled just outside city limits, and surely there were restaurants and shops near the museum for tourists to visit.

"But what about your ankle?" asked Jason.

"It hurts, but I think I can walk."

The boys helped me stand, and together we followed the road.

Chapter 42

A QUARTER OF A MILE later, we spotted a sign informing us that a Starbucks was nearby. Technically, we couldn't read the sign's Chinese writing, but the coffee shop's green and white logo was unmistakable.

"Who knew?" said Zac. "Even the Chinese like overpriced coffee."

Shortly thereafter, we entered Starbucks and placed an order: caramel macchiato, white chocolate mocha, iced tea, hot sandwiches, pastries, and yogurt. We were famished after our measly lunch and sprinting to flee from mercenaries. We sat at a corner table and waited for our food and drinks to be ready. The delicious scents of roasted coffee made the place feel cozy and warm.

Jason unzipped his backpack. He pulled out a phone charger, plugged in his phone, then removed a tablet and powered it on. "So what are we looking for?" he asked after logging into Starbucks' free Wi-Fi.

A barista called our name. Zac went to gather our food and drinks.

"I'm not sure," I said. "Dad asked if I remembered our vacation to Mexico City."

"When we visited the Teotihuacán ruins?"

I nodded.

Zac returned with our food and beverages. "You guys talking about our vacation to Mexico? That trip was the best."

Jason smiled. "Do you remember the fat man with the Chihuahua wearing a tiny sombrero?"

"Of course! How'd he get the Chihuahua to eat a taco like that?"

"Guys," I said. "Forget the inside jokes. Let's focus."

But the food smelled amazing, so instead of diving straight into researching Dad's cryptic message, we chowed down and didn't speak much. Once I finished the last of my strawberry yogurt with real fruit at the bottom, I wiped my mouth and motioned to Jason's tablet.

"Open Dad's Cloud account."

Zac looked from me to Jason. "How? You guys know his password?"

"Let's just say Dad's a brilliant historian—" Jason typed with his fingers onto the tablet's touchscreen, "—but he sucks with computers. I helped him set up his Cloud account."

"Not important," I said. "Do you have it pulled up?"

"Yeah," Jason swiveled his tablet so Zac and I could see its screen. A Google Drive account was opened. Files and documents were scattered everywhere.

"Ugh, I thought you helped Dad organize this thing."

"I did, but you know how he is."

We searched through countless files for nearly half an hour. Dad's Google Drive contained hundreds of documents, and its jumbled files made it confusing to navigate. Eventually, I saw a document titled: *Pictures of the Aztec Empire.*

"Hey, is that it?" I pointed at the file.

Jason looked at me like I was an idiot. "Do you remember nothing?"

"What?"

"Teotihuacán was a Mayan city. The Aztecs didn't make their appearance in history's records until much later."

"Well, *excuse* me, Mr. Brainiac."

"Don't call me that."

I rolled my eyes. "Keep looking."

He swiped to a new screen. I groaned. Another hundred files were placed haphazardly here as well. This could take days, possibly weeks, and we didn't have a clue what we were looking for.

I sat back and sighed. "This is hopeless."

"No," Jason sat up, excited. "I found it."

"Seriously? Just like that?"

"Look." He opened a file called *The Jones Family in Mexico.* Inside, hundreds of pictures and videos from our trip littered the screen. I couldn't believe how little Jason and Zac looked. It was embarrassing to see how chunky my cheeks were. In the colorful photographs, we visited beaches with white sand and turquoise water, swam in freezing underground cenotes, and climbed to the top of Mayan and Aztec pyramids. One of the videos, which appeared out of place because its thumbnail image showed a still shot of Dad's museum office, was titled *Birthplace of the gods.*

"What's that?" I asked.

"I dunno," said Jason. "Teotihuacán means birthplace of the gods, so this may be what Dad wanted us to find."

"Hit play."

Jason did. And the video that appeared onscreen made my heart drop to my stomach. The footage showed Dad in his museum office, wearing the same outfit we'd seen him in earlier tonight with Rico and his goons.

"Dad filmed this on the day he was kidnapped," I realized.

"*Shhh*," the boys hushed me.

Dad's hair was disheveled. He appeared to be sweating like he had run several miles and was still trying to catch his breath. His appearance isn't what alarmed me, however. It was the pistol in his hand.

"Since when has Dad ever owned a gun?" asked Zac.

Dad spoke, his voice frantic and winded. "I don't have much time, so listen carefully," he said. A loud bang sounded off-screen. Dad jumped, and his gaze darted toward his door just as another bang vibrated our speakers. It sounded like someone was trying to break into his office. He cocked the hammer of his pistol, then looked back into the camera. "Where to start? I guess at the beginning . . ."

Chapter 43

"IT BEGAN MORE THAN TWO thousand years ago," my father spoke quickly as another bang shook his office door and vibrated our tiny speakers. "The first emperor of China sought the Elixir of Life so he could live forever. But he failed to consider one thing.

"People wanted him dead."

Another bang, followed by indistinct shouting.

"Emperor Qin made many enemies. Not least among them was a young man whose father had been slain by the emperor's hands. The young man's father was a general in Emperor Qin's army. He helped defeat the emperor's rivals during the Warring States Period—"

Another bang. Splinters from the door went flying across the screen making my father flinch.

"Forget the history lesson. Here's what you need to know," he said. "Emperor Qin forced the general and all of his soldiers to drink a potion. The potion was supposed to make them invincible in battle. Instead, it turned them into terracotta." He paused for a second to let that sink in. "That's right, the terracotta warriors guarding Emperor Qin's tomb aren't statues—they're people. They are the general and his men. They've been cursed."

Another bang, and this time I flinched.

"The story doesn't stop there," he said. "The general's son disguised himself as an alchemist and presented the emperor with a potion he claimed to be the Elixir of Life. It was poison. But it was more than poison, it was something *else*." The bangs on the door were quickening. My dad's attackers must be about to break through. Even though I knew the video was pre-recorded, I felt my heart hammering in my chest.

"The potion is keeping him *alive*," my dad said. "Whoever drank the concoction would have eternal nightmares. Their soul would not rest. I fear if someone enters Emperor Qin's tomb and opens his sarcophagus, his body will rise from the grave. You heard me right, his corpse will awaken. We can't let that happen. I imagine after several millennia of nightmares he's gonna be pissed."

He pulled a piece of yellowing parchment out of his jacket pocket. "But there might be a way to stop him if that happens—"

The loudest bang yet sounded. My father looked up. His attackers broke through. Two mercenaries the size of pro football players charged into view. Dad raised his pistol and fired, fired—but his bullets pinged off their tactical assault gear. The mercenaries tackled him. The three of them went sprawling to the ground and out of the camera's view. I found myself trying to peer beyond the camera to see what was going on. Jason and Zac were glued to the screen, their faces white with fear. All I could hear was the sounds of struggle.

Then Dad popped into view and held the yellowing parchment up to the camera.

It was a crude drawing of a mechanism with levers and gears. Hastily scrawled in the corner were the words *General Li Fei* and *Acrobatics Pit.* There was also Chinese lettering and a sketch of a terracotta dancer, but before I could see more, Dad shoved the paper into his mouth.

"Cough it up!" bellowed the mercenary with a lumberjack beard. He put Dad into a headlock. My father's eyes bulged as he tried to swallow the evidence. Although he was in trouble, Dad reached out and smacked a key on his computer. A timer started ticking down with a three-second limit.

"He's destroying the hard drive," the second mercenary shouted, who looked like a bodybuilder with a chiseled jawline and a buzz cut of blond hair. He rushed to the computer while Dad struggled with Lumberjack.

Two, the timer counted down.

Bodybuilder jabbed computer keys.

One.

Dad passed out.

Zero.

The screen went black. The video was over.

Chapter 44

I GLANCED AT MY BROTHERS. Tears welled up in their eyes. I wiped my cheeks and noticed I was crying, too.

"We gotta go back and help him," said Zac.

"We will," I said.

Jason dried his eyes on the sleeve of his shirt. "How?" he asked. "Dad mentioned some pretty crazy stuff. You guys don't actually believe him, do you? I mean, his story is farfetched—the terracotta warriors are cursed and Emperor Qin is buried but *alive.* How is that possible, when archaeologists say the terracotta warriors were created in an assembly line process? The torsos, legs, and arms were created separately before being attached to the sculpted heads."

"Yeah, but you heard Dad," I said. "And he's the biggest skeptic we know. If he believes the terracotta warriors are mummies, then I do, too."

"It's just so unbelievable."

"But it would explain so much. For one, that's why all the statues look different—because they are different *people.*"

"I dunno . . ."

"It sounds ridiculous, I get it. But if Dad's story is real and the tomb is opened, then the evil spirit of Emperor Qin is going to be unleashed."

"Do you hear yourself, Maddie?" Jason tapped the table to emphasize his point. "Rico is after Qin's treasures. He wants the artifacts. Period. Corpses don't rise from graves, and terracotta warriors *aren't* people. You make it sound like they might awaken, too."

My eyes widened. "What if they *do*?"

Jason scoffed.

"No, hear me out," I said. "Dad's final message—the paper he held up to the screen—didn't it mention General Li Fei and an acrobatics pit? There was a drawing of a mechanism. What if the device is how we can awaken the terracotta warriors?"

"Why would we want to wake *them*?" asked Zac.

"Because I imagine they're pretty ticked at Emperor Qin for being forced to drink that potion. They might help us out if the emperor's sarcophagus is opened."

Jason waved my comments away.

None of us talked for several minutes. I sipped the last of my caramel macchiato, the syrup at the bottom sticky and yummy. If only I could convince my brother . . .

Zac finally spoke. "What'd we have to lose?"

"Everything," I answered. "We've already lost Mom . . ."

"Exactly," he said. "Dad's in trouble. Going back to the museum to search for that mechanism could be a chance to save him."

"Or it could be a fool's errand," said Jason.

"Shut up, Jason. We're going back. Stay if you want." I stood to leave.

"Wait," Jason placed his hand on my arm. "I'm sorry I don't believe in the supernatural—but that doesn't mean I'm not gonna help Dad."

"Are you coming with us, then?" I asked.

"Of course," he said.

"Then it sounds like we've got a mission," Zac said, smiling. "We'll sneak into the Museum of Terracotta Warriors without Rico's mercenaries spotting us, find the mechanism, and activate it. Should be easy enough."

"I don't think it's going to be that simple," Jason said, but he grinned. "Let's follow Dad's clue."

"Now we're talking," I said.

We high-fived.

I know. Cheesy. But our spirits were lifted with confidence as we hiked back to the Museum of Terracotta Warriors.

Chapter 45

I DIDN'T FEEL CONFIDENT ONCE we arrived. It neared midnight. The museum grounds were desolate and quiet. A spooky mist snaked its way through the gardens, thickening around the base of Emperor Qin's burial mound.

"Where's Rico and his goons?" asked Zac.

"Probably near the mound," said Jason, sweeping his phone's flashlight in that direction. "But without heavy-duty tractors and equipment, I have no idea how they'll unearth the tomb's entrance."

"I do," I said. "With the Shoemaker's scroll. It's a spell, remember?"

"Let's not start that supernatural nonsense again."

I pretended to zip my mouth shut and throw away the key. "Consider it ended. So where's this acrobatics pit Dad mentioned?"

Jason opened a small pocket in his backpack. He pulled out a folded map of the museum. If you've ever been to a theme park like Disney or Universal, then you'll get an idea of what this map looked like—a colorful cartoon version of the park, complete with icons representing the various sites, picnic tables, and bathrooms. I vaguely recalled Jason grabbing the map right before we started our tour this morning.

"Surrounding the mound are various pits," Jason said as he unfolded the map, shining his light on the crinkly paper. "Archaeologists discovered warriors at each site—well, all except the acrobatics pit. The acrobatics pit contained what is believed to be Emperor Qin's royal burial court—complete with dancers and acrobats to provide him with entertainment in the afterlife.

"Most of the statues archaeologists discovered at the site were destroyed, crushed beneath the weight of dirt and rock. They moved them to exhibit galleries and reassembled the pieces."

"You mean they reassembled the bones," said Zac.

Jason shook his head. "They're statues, not people."

"Mummies," I corrected.

"I thought you said you were through?"

"Oops," I smirked.

"Whatever, I'm not sure what's left in the pit now."

We crept across the desolate grounds for nearly twenty minutes, moving slowly and cautiously as Jason led the way using his map. Every so often, he stopped to check the map for signs we traveled in the right direction. We were lucky—no mercenaries patrolled the grounds, and the only life we saw were bats swooping down to catch mosquitos. Then, after I was beginning to think we'd never reach the acrobatics pit, we found it.

"Fetch," I swore. "There's nothing here."

The acrobatics pit was just a rectangular hole dug out of the earth. Ropes were laid over the site in a grid pattern to help archaeologists explore every grain of dirt. It was simply a lame dig site. I'd seen hundreds of them traveling with

Dad. We didn't see the mechanism we searched for, no levers or gears.

Zac grabbed a handful of dirt and threw it. "Well, this is a load of malarkey."

"Malarkey?" I said.

"What? If feels like a malarkey moment."

"It's never a malarkey moment, Zac."

Jason hopped down into the pit to search around for clues. I sat on the edge of the pit and scratched my head. "I don't get it," I said. "The message Dad wrote on that yellowing paper looked like it said acrobatics pit. Did we misread it?"

"Nah, I read the same thing," said Jason, stepping over gridded ropes as he shined his light around the site.

"Then what have we missed? Everything Dad discovered so far has been true—like how his map pointed us to the Shoemaker."

"What if there are more clues on Dad's map?" Zac suggested. "It has so many tiny details, and with its writing in Chinese except for Dad's notes, the parchment may have hidden messages."

Jason swept his light toward Zac. "That's actually a brilliant idea."

"Who knew?" I said. "Zac's a sleuth."

"Hey, I'm not slow," he protested.

"I didn't say sloth, Zac. I said *sleuth*—you know, like a detective."

"Oh . . ."

Smirking, I pulled Dad's map from my pocket. There wasn't enough light to see it clearly, so Jason tossed me his phone. I caught it in mid-air, then I shone its light on the yellowing parchment. I searched the parchment for hidden words or secret writing. Nothing stood out beyond what we'd already read. The maze of tunnels, all organized around a central circle, seemed to be the goal—the place where Emperor Qin's sarcophagus might be laid to rest. Within the circle, I noticed a tiny drawing of a three-geared device and a lever.

Wait, the drawing matched the sketch of a mechanism from Dad's video.

I showed my brothers the discovery.

"But what does it mean?" asked Zac.

I thought for a moment. "How many acrobat statues did archaeologists discover at this site?"

Jason shrugged. "Maybe a dozen or so."

"Doesn't sound like much of a royal court, does it?" I pointed out. "I mean, think about it. Qin has thousands of warriors, but only a few entertainers? Wouldn't he have hundreds of them?"

"I guess so . . ."

"But if the royal burial court isn't here," said Zac. "Where is it?"

I pointed at the map and placed my finger in the center of the maze. "Here," I said.

Zac turned to look at the large hill silhouetted in the distance. "Inside the tomb?"

"Exactly," I said. "Qin's royal burial court is inside the tomb with him. Which means the mechanism we're looking for is there as well."

"This changes things," Jason said.

"Definitely," I agreed.

No sooner had we come to this realization, when a flash of green light flared from the base of the mound. An explosion boomed. The ground quaked. I whirled toward the noise and saw black smoke billowing into the air.

Then somebody screamed. Gunshots rang out.

The hairs on the back of my neck stood on end. I glanced at my brothers, my heart pounding as more gunfire erupted. Flashes of light from muzzle blasts could be seen in the distance.

"What the fetch is happening over there?" said Zac.

I swallowed, trying not to imagine Dad being shot by mercenaries or being blown to smithereens.

Jason voiced a thought I hadn't yet considered. "I think Emperor Qin's tomb has just been opened."

Chapter 46

THE GUNSHOTS CEASED. Whatever the mercenaries fired at was either dead, or maybe they'd simply gotten spooked—I wasn't sure. No bullets came whizzing past our heads, so I felt confident the attack hadn't been aimed at us. Nonetheless, the din of assault rifles unnerved me.

Jason climbed out of the pit. "We gotta check it out."

"Are you nuts?" I said. "Did you hear the gunfire?"

"Yeah, but what if something happened to Dad?"

I swallowed to calm my nerves. As much as I hated to admit it, Jason was right. We needed to find out if Dad was okay. "All right," I breathed. "Let's sneak over there and see what's going on."

We crept closer toward the large mound as black smoke curled into the air. Unusual green light illuminated the area. We stalked through shadows and hid behind trees to mask our approach. Images of Dad lying injured with blood pooling beneath him flashed across my mind—and I quickened my pace. We reached the base of the mound and knelt behind a garden of bushes, then we peeked out for a better look.

I gasped.

The side of the hill had been blown away. But whatever caused the blast couldn't have been TNT or dynamite because everything looked . . . unnatural. Glowing scorch marks scarred the mound. They looked like veins of lightning streaked through the dirt, silver and luminescent. The strange markings expanded outward from the source of the blast—a set of massive bronze doors embedded into the hillside.

The doors were open.

Inside, flickering torchlight illuminated the foyer, but the torches emitted green flames instead of natural fire. The torches rested in metallic sconces hanging on stone walls. They gave the tomb's entrance a ghostly glow and made shadows shift unnaturally. A hallway stretched deeper into the mound.

I shivered. "It looks like an entrance to the Underworld."

"What's that?" asked Zac.

I looked to where he pointed. Lying on the ground between the doors was . . . something. It looked like a body—a corpse. My heart rose to my throat.

Zac choked back a sob. "Dad . . ."

The sound of a gun cocking came from behind.

"Do not move," somebody spoke, the person's English accented heavily with Mandarin. "Hands up. Turn 'round, slowly."

We did as instructed.

I expected to see Zheng and his tattooed hand. Instead, we found Mr. Yao—Tamora's limousine driver—looming over us with a revolver aimed at my head.

Chapter 47

"TÀITÀI ROSE!" SHOUTED MR. YAO. "I caught them!"

Tamora emerged from the shadows. She wore gray cargo pants, a black blouse, and a mini-Glock pistol was gripped in her hand. The sight of Tamora—armed—startled me.

"Goodness, Mr. Yao," Tamora purred. "Don't aim your gun at the children."

"Oh, my apologies, Tàitài Rose." He lowered his weapon.

I released the breath I'd been holding. It quivered on the exhale.

Tamora grabbed my arm and squeezed. "What's wrong with you, child? You were instructed to stay at the hotel until I arrived."

"Ow—Tamora—you're hurting me."

She looked down at her hand squeezing my arm, and let go. "Well," she said. "What do you kids have to say for yourselves?"

"S-sorry," the boys said together in dull tones.

"Tamora, we found Dad," I said.

"Enough with your lies, Maddie!"

Jason stepped forward. "No, she's telling the truth. We saw him."

Tamora arched a blond eyebrow. "You did? When? Where?"

"Tonight," I said. "He was kidnapped by a man named Rico Raja. The guy has mercenaries and everything. They went inside the tomb."

Tamora glanced at the tomb's entrance. Her eyes darted from the open tomb doors to the body, to the unnatural green light and the silvery lightning veins streaking outward in every direction. "Bloody hell," she swore. "Hank has stepped into a world of trouble this time, hasn't he?"

I nodded, not knowing what else to say.

"All right, kids—" she sighed, checking her pistol to make sure a bullet was loaded into the chamber "—stay close. This may get bumpy."

Minutes later, we hiked through the brush to reach the tomb's entrance. I felt lightheaded as we approached the body. What if it really was Dad? We tiptoed toward the corpse, which was lying face down, but I found I couldn't go any closer. Its hair color was the same as Dad's. Tears welled up in my eyes and blurred my vision.

Tamora shoved the body onto its back with the heel of her black combat boot. The corpse's face was revealed . . .

. . . and I let out a much-needed sigh.

It wasn't Dad.

It was a dead mercenary.

The mercenary's eyes stared tirelessly forward, death face contorted in pain. Whatever killed him didn't do it gently. Blood leaked from his eyes like tears. Clenched in his fist was a small, rolled parchment.

Jason crept closer.

"What are you doing?" Zac demanded.

"Something's in his hand."

"Careful," Tamora warned. "The tomb's entrance must've been booby-trapped."

Jason paused to consider her words. Then, resigned to retrieve the parchment, he knelt and grabbed it carefully, slowly.

He groaned. "It's the Shoemaker's scroll."

"Do you believe me now?" I asked.

"What?" said Tamora.

I explained what we'd overheard Zheng telling Rico about the scroll—how it was a Wǔshén spell designed to open the tomb. I expected her to bat her eyes. Instead, her gaze shifted to the tomb's entrance and the unnatural green glow emanating from within.

"This is a dangerous place," she mumbled.

"What killed him?" asked Jason.

"Dark magic," Tamora answered.

"You can't be serious."

She motioned to the dead mercenary. "Do you see any markings of what killed him?"

Jason shook his head.

"We heard gunfire," Zac told her. "Maybe he was shot."

"Unlikely," Tamora said. "The mercenaries were firing at something else."

"Yeah, but what?"

"Something *else*—" she said with importance.

Mr. Yao finally spoke, in Mandarin this time. His tone was frantic.

"Yes, I know the tomb is cursed," Tamora responded in English. "And since you refuse to go any farther, I suggest you go and prepare the car. Be ready to leave at a minute's notice."

Mr. Yao bowed, then departed in a hurry.

Tamora turned her attention to us. "All right, children, let's go get your father." And she led us inside the booby-trapped tomb.

Chapter 48

WE EACH GRABBED A TORCH with green flames and descended deeper into Emperor Qin's tomb. The ghostly light illuminated a cobblestone walkway, stone walls, and a low arched ceiling. The air felt warmer the farther we went, our footsteps echoing around us. Sweat beaded on my brow and my skin felt clammy. It smelled musty—a stench mingled with staleness that came from places unoccupied for a long time.

We reached a fork in the path.

The tunnel we'd been hiking for the past several minutes continued onward into the gloom, but now we had a decision to make. Did we press forward, or turn left with this new branching tunnel?

"What does Dad's map say?" asked Jason.

I unfolded the yellowing parchment and brought my torchlight closer so I could read its details. Tamora and the boys huddled around me. Together we studied the map in flickering green light, the unnatural fire crackling.

"It looks like we entered here," Tamora pointed.

"So that would mean we're here." I motioned to a spot where the tunnel split in two directions. It looked like the tunnel going straight ran into a dead end.

We all looked up from the map to stare down the left tunnel. Its stone walls curved inward and disappeared around a bend. If we were reading Dad's map correctly, then we were about to travel into the outermost tunnel of a circular maze.

"Do any of you have a pen?" I asked.

"No, why?" asked Jason.

"So we can mark on Dad's map where we've been. Otherwise, we're going to get lost."

"Here." Tamora handed me a tube of red lipstick. "Use that, love."

"Thanks." I uncapped the lipstick and painted an X on Dad's map to indicate the maze's beginning. Then I pocketed the lipstick and started to lead the way down the tunnel—

—when a blast sounded in the distance. The walls rumbled. Sand and dust fell from the ceiling and landed in my hair.

"What was that?" asked Zac.

"It sounded like explosives," Tamora said.

"It must be Rico and his men," Jason said. "They are probably blowing up walls to make their own path through the maze."

"Even more reason to tread lightly," Tamora said.

We traveled down the left tunnel. It didn't take long for choices to emerge regarding which way to go. More tunnels branched out, most of them snaking inward to the center of the maze. I gave directions using the map. We turned right. Then left. Straight this time. The place was disorienting. Even with the map and Tamora's lipstick to mark our path, the labyrinthine passageways were confusing. More than once we had to retrace our steps because I led us to a dead end.

Eventually, we reached a tunnel choked with smoke and dust—the first signs that Rico and his men had been this way. A hole had been blown in the wall and stone debris littered the ground.

"Should we follow the destruction?" asked Zac.

"I think so," Tamora said.

"But did they go left or right after blowing up the wall?"

We stepped through the hole and peered down the passageways, but it was difficult to see beyond the haze of smoke. I studied Dad's map and recommended that we take the path leading left, so we navigated through the debris and went in that direction. The tunnel led to a large chamber the size of a school gymnasium.

"This room isn't on Dad's map," I informed.

"That's worrying," Tamora said.

We entered the room. As our torchlight illuminated the space in hues of green, I gasped at what I saw. It was the most magnificent room I'd ever seen. It appeared the entire space was a miniature model of Emperor Qin's China as it must have looked 2,000 years ago. As I scanned the ground I saw palaces, villages, forests, and rivers of mercury flowing through mountains of bronze. Overhead, the ceiling mimicked the nighttime sky, with precious gemstones embedded into the ceiling to represent stars and constellations.

Tamora gasped, clearly in awe of this discovery. I imagined a room like this would be every archaeologist's wildest dream.

"It's an underground kingdom," said Jason.

"Yeah, but where do we go from here?" asked Zac.

Now that he mentioned it, I realized the chamber had no exits other than the one we had just entered through. Glancing at the map didn't help since the room wasn't shown amongst the labyrinthine passageways, but if I had pinpointed our location on the map correctly, then a tunnel should be located beyond this room. But where was it? Hidden behind a wall?

An explosion sounded in the distance back the way we came. The chamber quaked. Sand rained down from the ceiling of constellations.

"We must turn around," Tamora said. "The mercenaries didn't come this way."

We started to retreat from the chamber, but as I stepped backward my foot depressed into the floor. A *click* sounded. I looked down to find the stone tile beneath my Converse high-top sunken lower than the other tiles. I lifted my foot and the stone tile rose back up—followed by a loud bang that sounded from deep inside the walls. The chamber began to rumble.

"I didn't do it," I said. "I swear the stone pressed in on its own!"

Stone grinded against stone—and the open doorway we had entered through suddenly rumbled closed as a bronze door lowered from the arched opening.

"NO!" Tamora rushed to the closing door, but it shut before she could get there. It closed with a resounding thud. Dust shot up from the ground.

The torches in our hands sputtered out. We were thrust into darkness so black I couldn't even see my hand waving before my eyes.

"Was that supposed to happen?" I breathed into the dark.

"Dunno," I heard Jason say.

The torches flickered back to life, but now their flames were purple.

"Whoa, look at that!" said Zac, pointing our attention to the model of China. Beneath our feet, the flowing rivers of mercury began to slowly rise. A toxic gas filled the chamber, misting out from the huts and palaces.

"I hate to be the bearer of bad news, loves," Tamora said. "But we have only moments to live."

Chapter 49

I INHALED A DEEP BREATH and felt a sharp pang in my chest. The back of my throat itched, making me cough. Tamora and the boys began coughing, too.

"The gas is poisonous!" yelled Tamora. "Hold your breath and search for a way out! There must be a secret lever or switch!"

We went in different directions. I filled my lungs with air, suppressed the sudden urge to cough, and held it. Then I stepped over a bronze mountain that came up to my knees and searched the miniature model of China on the floor. Everywhere I looked the model included tiny details: campfires made of polished amber, early construction of the Great Wall on its outskirts, villages, and huts with white mist vaping from their chimneys. I knelt beside a tiny village in the shade of a bronze mountain and felt around for secret buttons. I pushed down on hills and rooftops and bridges, but nothing pressed in.

Across the chamber, Tamora found grooves in a wall in the shape of a door. She ran her hands along its edges looking for a switch, but with no luck. She shoved her shoulder into it—but the door wouldn't give.

"Dad's map!" Jason shouted.

I unfolded the parchment with fumbling fingers. I tried to read Dad's notes, but my lungs screamed for air and I felt like I might faint. The purple torchlight cast dimmer light than the green torches had, so I held the map closer to its flame so I could get a better look.

What the fetch!

A watermark was hidden in the parchment, only visible when held up to the purple flame. There were four creatures at each edge of the parchment: a tiger, phoenix, tortoise, and dragon. The tortoise was located at the top of the page, the phoenix at the bottom, tiger on the left, and dragon on the right.

What did the symbols mean?

Poisonous gas continued flooding into the chamber. Its mist created a deadly fog that threatened to swallow the miniature model of China on the floor. The rivers of mercury rose higher and higher.

I stole a breath and regretted it immediately. The taste of ozone filled my mouth and clung to the back of my throat, making me cough. My head felt fuzzy. I raised my torchlight higher to illuminate more of the model, and something nearby gleamed.

It was a blue pebble fitted perfectly inside of a niche recessed into a mountainside. I hurried to the pebble and scooped it up. Nothing happened inside the chamber, but my find seemed significant.

"I found something!" I shouted, inhaling another gulp of air. Lightheadedness made me dizzy.

Tamora, Jason, and Zac rushed to my side. I showed them my discovery of the blue stone, and held my torch near the map to show them the watermark. Zac revealed something in his hand. It was a pebble the same shape and size as mine, only white.

"What do the rocks mean?" asked Jason. He coughed.

"It's a puzzle," Tamora said. "In Chinese astronomy, the azure dragon represents the east while the white tiger represents the west." She pointed at Dad's map, and showed us how the watermarked dragon was located on the right side of the parchment, the east, while the tiger was located on the left, the west. "They are cardinal directions. The colored stones represent each animal. Where did you find your stone, Maddie?"

I motioned to the mountains.

"There aren't many mountains west of China. It's mostly deserts," Tamora pointed out. "The stones are out of place, meaning—"

"We have to match them up," I realized.

"Precisely, love."

"But how?" said Zac. "We're underground. We don't know which way is north."

I showed him my compass necklace.

"Brilliant," Tamora said. "All right, the dragon is azure. So the blue stone goes . . ."

I checked my compass. "There!" I pointed eastward.

Jason grabbed my blue stone, and rushed to an area of the model that looked like a coastline. He searched around until he found a niche the pebble went inside. He knelt into the mist and emerged holding a black stone.

"The black turtle—*coff, coff*—is north," Tamora informed.

Jason darted off to set the black stone. He hopped the Great Wall and disappeared into the mist. At the same time, Zac rushed to place the white stone into a niche inside of the mountainside. The red stone was already in the correct location nestled between villages near the southern sea.

As soon as the last pebble was fitted into place, the sound of misting gasses ceased as toxic fumes stopped vaping from chimneys. The rivers of mercury lowered. A stone wall rumbled into the floor, revealing a hidden passageway. And we rushed out of the chamber, coughing and gasping for air.

Chapter 50

I LEANED AGAINST A WALL outside the chamber, gasping. The back of my throat felt hoarse from breathing in poisonous gasses, and water leaked from my eyes. The stale tomb air tasted sweeter than anything I'd ever known.

Zac coughed. "Dad's map did say not to open the tomb."

"He wasn't joking." Jason wiped bleary eyes on the sleeve of his jacket. "We almost died like Emperor Qin."

I arched an eyebrow. "What'd you mean?"

"Qin feared death," he explained, "so he sought the Elixir of Life believing the potion could grant him immortality. He even hired alchemists who promised they could make the Elixir . . ."

"He died after drinking mercury," Tamora cut him short, sweeping past us to march down the new tunnel. "Hence the rivers of mercury in the chamber. The Ancients were obsessed with the stuff."

I caught up to her. "Do you think something else could've been mixed in his drink?"

"Like what, dear?"

I thought about Dad's video message and his story of Emperor Qin's mysterious death. "Like poison or something else."

"It's possible," she acknowledged, but she turned her attention to her mini-Glock pistol and checked its chamber. The sight of her gun reminded me that we faced more than deadly tomb traps, but also mercenaries prepared to kill.

We stopped talking. This was a dangerous place. I mean, we nearly died for crying out loud. Plus it was probably better to keep quiet anyways. The last thing we needed was to announce our presence stupidly to mercenaries.

For the next twenty minutes, we roamed the new maze of tunnels in complete silence. I occasionally whispered directions as I navigated with Dad's map. Our torches sputtered and snapped, their flames once again flickering green. A droning *drip, drip, drip* echoed from somewhere far ahead.

"It doesn't appear Rico's goons came this way," Jason whispered into the gloom.

"I was thinking the same thing," said Zac. "We haven't seen any blown-up walls."

"That's okay, loves," Tamora said. "Tombs are labyrinths with many possible routes to the main burial chamber. We will find your father."

I knew Tamora spoke from experience. She had accompanied Dad on numerous digs throughout the years and raided countless tombs.

We crept through the maze for another half-hour with only our thoughts to occupy the time. It was hard to believe where we were—deep beneath the earth in a place no one had walked for 2,000 years. If this wasn't a life or death situation I might have enjoyed our adventure.

The sound of dripping water grew louder. It seemed the map was leading us closer to its source. Eventually, we reached a circular chamber. The room was half the size of the last one with a domed ceiling and a cobblestone floor. This chamber didn't house a miniature model of China. Instead, a stream of silver mercury *dripped* from a hole in the ceiling and landed in a ceramic goblet sitting on a raised pedestal in the center of the room. Mercury overflowed the goblet's rim, pooled atop the pedestal, and spilled onto the floor. At the edges of the round chamber were four additional pedestals, each carved to resemble one of the cardinal direction animals.

Zac gulped. "This doesn't look promising."

"No, but it explains a lot," Tamora said. She must have noticed my puzzled expression, because she added, "Chinese archaeologists discovered heavy traces of mercury in the soil samples they collected from the mound."

"Ah," I said. "But how do we get past this chamber? I don't see it on Dad's map, and it appears there should be a spiraling tunnel located here."

"We'll have to go inside to investigate," Tamora said. "The question is . . . are you willing to risk your life to go deeper inside the tomb?"

The logical part of my brain screamed, *No, run away and preserve your life!* But my heart spoke a softer yet stronger message: *Dad needs you.* So I stepped into the room. The boys followed me inside. Tamora was the last to enter.

As soon as she stepped inside, the entrance rumbled as a bronze door lowered from the arched opening. None of us raced to escape before it closed. It banged with a solid thud, sealing us within. Dust shot up. Our green torches snuffed out and transformed to purple.

"The flames," I said, understanding their significance. "They change colors when we have to overcome a trial."

"Well, let's pray this trial isn't our last," said Jason.

Chapter 51

I STUDIED THE CHAMBER AND its contents. The room appeared to be another puzzle. My eyes followed the mercury dripping from the ceiling to land in a ceramic goblet. The goblet sat on a stone pedestal in the center of the room. Four more stone pedestals were located along the walls of the circular chamber. Each one had been carved to resemble an animal from Chinese astronomy and painted: a white tiger, a red phoenix, a black tortoise, and a blue dragon.

"What does all of this mean?" I asked.

Tamora crept cautiously toward the pedestal carved like a white tiger. She knelt and inspected the pedestal while shining her purple torchlight. I moved toward the pedestal carved like a blue dragon, careful of my footing in case a stone tile turned out to be a hidden switch. We didn't need another death trap sprung on us from a clumsy mistake. My torchlight illuminated the pedestal's intricately carved design. Its flat top had an etching of grapes on a leafy vine.

"Interesting," Tamora mumbled.

"What'd you find?" I asked.

"Stars are decorated on this pedestal's tabletop."

"Mine's different. It has grapes."

Tamora pointed at the other pedestals. "What about those two?"

The boys inspected the pedestals. "Stars," they said together.

"So one of them is different . . ."

Curious if Dad's map offered clues, I held it up to the purple torchlight, but nothing new stood out. As far as I could tell, this room's puzzle didn't come with a watermark or hidden symbol to help us solve the riddle.

"What'd we do?" asked Zac, a tinge of nervousness in his voice.

Tamora motioned to the ceramic goblet resting on the center pedestal—which I noticed was plain and didn't have any etchings carved on its surface. "The cup must be the key."

Something Jason said earlier suddenly hit me. "Qin drank mercury, right? Did the Chinese also drink wine?"

Tamora nodded. "They drank huangjiu—a yellow wine. It's been around for thousands of years."

"Then perhaps we must set the goblet of mercury onto the dragon pedestal since it has grapes."

Jason moved cautiously toward the goblet. "That would make sense. Qin likely drank his elixir from a similar goblet. Wait, what if this goblet is the same one he drank from— the one that killed him?"

"Then that would be *extremely* ironic," I said. "Because it might kill us."

Zac groaned.

"Tamora . . . what do you think?"

She considered our situation for a moment. "I think you may be right, Maddie. Let's move the goblet to the dragon pedestal and see what happens."

Jason was closest to the goblet. He lifted the cup using both hands and tried not to spill any of the mercury. Immediately, the pedestal the cup had been sitting on shook, twisted, and rumbled a foot lower. A bone-chilling shriek filled the chamber. Overhead, slits opened in the ceiling.

And deadly white spikes appeared looking like sharpened bone.

They descended slowly into the chamber, threatening to impale us. There were dozens of them. No space in the room would be spared.

"Are you serious?!" I groaned. "We don't have time for this Indiana Jones bullcrap."

"*Move, move!*" shouted Tamora. "*Place the goblet on the pedestal!*"

Jason darted to the dragon pedestal and set the goblet on its surface. The pedestal shook and mercury sloshed about, then the pedestal sank a foot into the floor. The other pedestals did, too.

But nothing else happened.

The spikes kept lowering.

"What'd we miss?!" I demanded.

"The cardinal directions!" Jason said, his voice frantic.

"He's right," said Tamora. "The pedestals must be out of sync with north and south."

"Holy fetch, guys! We're gonna die!" Zac clawed fingers through his hair as he stared at the spikes of bone. They were now a few feet away from the tops of our heads.

I grabbed my compass necklace and checked which direction was north. "Okay, got it!" I said. "We need to push all four pedestals counterclockwise ninety degrees to match them up with their directions."

"How?" asked Jason. "They're made of stone!"

Zac stopped staring at the sharpened bones to point our attention to the base of the rounded walls. "When the pedestals lowered a track appeared. They're resting on top of it."

"That was news we needed to know yesterday, Zac!"

"Sorry, but I'm kinda freaking out right now!"

"Everyone get a pedestal," Tamora instructed. "Push on three. One—two—"

But we all started pushing before she finished counting. My dragon pedestal slid along the wall, its stone base grinding against the track. Mercury sloshed about. I tried to measure my steps in terms of degrees, counting aloud as we pushed. As we got closer to ninety, the spikes were nearly on top of us.

We matched the pedestals up with their cardinal directions.

But still, nothing happened.

"The goblet!" shouted Jason.

Oh, fetch! Most of the mercury spilled out. The goblet was only half-full.

I scooped the cup into my hand, rushed to the center pedestal where mercury spilled onto the floor, and held it up to the silver liquid.

"Hurry!"

The spikes were only three feet from the ground. All of us were squatting to avoid being impaled. Mercury now filled the goblet to the rim. Trying not to panic, I crawled back to the dragon pedestal with cold mercury dripping onto my hands. Then, praying we solved the puzzle correctly, I placed the goblet of mercury onto the pedestal's surface.

A strange hissing sounded. The dragon pedestal began to sink, right out of sight, leaving a large pipe exposed—a pipe wide enough for a man to slide into.

I heard Zac gasp and looked up. The spikes weren't stopping.

"Everybody down there, now!" yelled Tamora.

White-faced, the boys reached the opening and leapt into the pipe head first. They slid out of sight.

"Now you, Maddie!"

I quickly lowered myself into the pipe legs first, then let go.

Chapter 52

I RUSHED DOWN A SLIMY, spiraling, dark pipe that reminded me of a tube slide at a waterpark. Wind brushed my cheeks and raked through my hair. The pipe twisted and turned, sloping steeply downward. Behind me, I could hear Tamora thumping into the curves. I wondered what would happen when we hit the bottom. What if more spikes awaited us? Or a hundred-foot drop to a slab of cold stone?

But the pipe leveled out.

I shot out of the end and skidded across a wet cobblestone floor before coming to a stop. Looking around, I saw we'd emerged in a dark tunnel with a stone archway ceiling tall enough to stand in. Jason and Zac were getting to their feet. Both of them were covered in gray slime. The same sludge covered me from head to toe, reeking of sewer water boiling in the sun. I stood to my feet and flung some of the nasty muck out of my hair—just as Tamora came shooting out of the pipe. I jumped aside and she thumped and rolled across the cobblestones.

"How deep are we beneath the mound?" asked Zac, squinting around at our dark surroundings. His voice echoed off the damp walls.

"Miles, probably," said Jason.

"It's so dark."

"I've got a light." Jason turned on his phone's flashlight and it lit up the tunnel. Cockroaches and centipedes skittered into cracks and beneath heaps of sludge to avoid the brightness. The sight of bugs made me shudder.

Jason directed his light down the tunnel. The damp stone walls glistened. All four of us turned to stare ahead, where the tunnel branched out in several directions.

Tamora flung slime from her clothes. "C'mon, kids," she said. "We must be close to the maze's center by now."

I double-checked the map to find where the spiraling tunnel slide ended, then off we went, our footsteps slapping in puddles on the wet floor. The tunnel was so dark, and Jason's cell phone light made our shadows look monstrous on the walls, but we navigated the lower tunnels of the maze without much trouble.

Tamora led us forward with her pistol gripped tightly in both hands. "If you see mercenaries," she warned us. "Get behind me."

But we didn't see anyone. And the tunnels were as quiet as a midnight cemetery. The first sound we heard startled us—a loud *crunch* as Zac stepped on something. Jason lowered his light so we could look at the floor. It was littered with the molted shedding of giant scorpion husks the size of human skulls. There must have been hundreds of them. I gulped, hoping the giant scorpions these exoskeletons once belonged to were no longer alive.

The curve of our dark tunnel straightened out.

"Guys, I see something up ahead—" said Zac, grabbing my shoulder.

I froze, watching. I could just see the outline of a chamber's huge, curved opening. Inside, purple firelight flickered and made shadows dance.

"Maybe it's the burial chamber," I breathed, glancing at the others. My heart beat so fast it hurt.

Then someone shouted from the chamber: "Open the sarcophagus!"

"No—whoever opens that coffin will die!"

My stomach lurched. That sounded like Dad. Throwing caution to the wind, I shouldered past Tamora and raced ahead.

"Maddie, wait!"

I didn't stop. Dad's life was in danger. My legs carried me forward, shoes sloshing across wet cobblestone, and my mind raced with a frightening revelation.

My nightmare was about to come true.

Chapter 53

I SLIPPED QUIETLY INTO THE chamber. It was a massive room with a domed ceiling at least thirty feet high supported by four red pillars the size of redwood trees. I crouched in the shadows behind one of the pillars, and peered ahead. Hundreds of terracotta statues filled the space: acrobatics, dancers, and Emperor Qin's concubines—women who must have been his lovers in life. The concubine statues were scantily clothed, wearing red robes and hardly anything else.

Here and there, a treasury of riches sat on pedestals scattered throughout the room. Mounds of treasure were heaped on the floor: piles of precious gemstones sparkling in purple torchlight, golden goblets, jewelry, and countless coins with little squares hollowed out in their centers.

This was Qin's burial court.

Tamora and the boys crept up behind me. I held a finger to my mouth signaling them to remain quiet, then we began spying. Across the way, I saw a hole blasted into the wall where Rico and his men forced their way in. At least a dozen mercenaries—along with Rico, Zheng, and Lynch—stood in the center of the room with purple torches held in their hands. My father was amongst them, but he was held at gunpoint. It appeared everyone argued over a richly decorated item at the heart of the chamber.

A golden sarcophagus inlaid with emeralds, jades, and rubies.

The final resting place of the First Qin Emperor, I thought.

"If we open this sarcophagus everybody might die," my dad was saying.

"Do not listen to him," Zheng told Rico. "You wish for immortality, do you not? The Scroll of Everlasting Life is inside. Open the coffin. See for yourself."

Rico ignored my father's warning. He stepped closer to the sarcophagus and rested his hands on its surface. "Eternal life," he breathed.

"Rico—listen to me—" my dad pleaded. "It's not what you think—"

"*Silence!*" Rico roared. "You do not understand, Dr. Jones. I have no choice. My daughter will die without this scroll . . ."

"Open the coffin," Zheng encouraged.

That's when my dad did something completely stupid. He punched Rico in the jaw. Rico reeled from the blow, stumbling back, and Dad grabbed one of his holstered pistols. Then he seized Rico in a chokehold like a human shield, and aimed the gun at his head.

"I can't let you do that," he said.

Chapter 54

MERCENARIES RAISED THEIR WEAPONS and pointed them at my dad.

"Lower your weapons or I'll kill your boss!" Dad yelled, but the mercenaries didn't listen. They kept aiming their guns. Lynch snickered. He seemed to be enjoying the chaos.

"And to think, Dr. Jones," Rico grimaced. "I thought you were wise—*nggh!*"

Dad struck him in the head with the butt of his pistol.

I felt like I might vomit. There was no way Dad could survive this. If the mercenaries didn't kill him, then Rico surely would if he was set free. Behind me, I heard the faintest whimper coming from Zac. Jason fumed and fidgeted, looking like he might run to Dad's aid any second. Meanwhile, Tamora eased to the edge of our pillar, pistol raised, and she did the bravest thing I'd ever seen a woman do.

She stepped out into the open.

"I'd do what he says," she spoke to the mercenaries. She aimed her Glock at Zheng. He watched her enter the chamber with a sort of maniacal glee. His firearm was still holstered on his hip and his tattooed hand rested beside the weapon. He made no move for the gun.

"Tamora," breathed Dad. "What on earth are you doing here?"

"Saving your butt, it seems."

"Well, I've never been happier to see you."

Tamora moved closer toward Dad and Rico, her gun never leaving her target. The mercenaries kept aiming their assault rifles. It was a Mexican standoff, guns pointed all over the room. I felt hopeless hiding with the boys. But what could we do? We were unarmed kids. The bad guys were all soldiers ready to kill.

Tamora reached Dad and now stood beside him. I expected the two of them to begin backing out of the chamber toward us—but instead, Tamora did something that made my stomach lurch.

She turned her aim on Dad, placing her Glock directly against his temple. "I'm sorry, Hank," she said. "But Rico is right . . . the emperor's sarcophagus must be opened."

Chapter 55

"HAND OVER YOUR GUN, HANK."

Dad gritted his teeth. He still held Rico in a chokehold. His eyes darted all over the room. I knew his calculating mind must be working through scenarios, trying to determine the best course of action.

"Don't make me pull the trigger."

"Tamora—why?"

Tamora snorted. She glanced at Zheng. "I've brought the children," she said. "They're hiding behind the pillars."

"What the fetch is she doing?" I said.

Zheng motioned to Lynch, who adjusted his eyepatch and led mercenaries toward our location. I turned to my brothers—their faces pleading, looking at me as though needing direction. But yet again, I didn't know what to do. Usually, in situations out of my control, the best decision was to run and deal with the consequences later.

"Back to the tunnel!" I yelled.

We sprinted toward the passageway we had entered from—

—but mercenaries appeared from around the other side of the pillar. Jason and Zac ran straight into them. They were seized immediately. I stopped in my tracks and turned around. Lynch was there to greet me with a nasty grin.

"We must stop meeting like this," he growled.

Then he grabbed a handful of my hair and yanked back hard. My head snapped toward his grubby hand. I cried out in pain and clawed at his hand to try and release his grip, but the mercenary was too strong. He dragged me, kicking and screaming, back into the chamber. My brothers were dragged in behind me, both of them shouting and fighting to break free.

Rico chuckled, still held hostage as a human shield. "Wonderful, Tamora. You shall be handsomely rewarded."

"I don't want your money," she said. "I just want my revenge."

"Tamora, you witch!" I screamed. "We trusted you!"

"Hush, child," she said, turning her attention to my dad. "Now, Hank—you murdering piece of garbage—surrender and give Rico the gun."

Dad's expression was one of horror. It seemed he struggled to comprehend Tamora's betrayal, and the sudden capture of his children by deadly mercenaries. His eyes met mine, and I could see in his gaze that his resolve was weakening. He released the chokehold on Rico.

Freed, Rico popped his neck left and right. He snatched the pistol from my father's grasp, then punched him in the stomach. "That was foolish, Dr. Jones."

Dad doubled over, coughing. "Tamora—" he panted. "How could you?"

Tamora scoffed, as though the reason for her betrayal should be obvious. "Do you not remember Atahualpa?"

"The Inca mummy of Ecuador?" Dad said. "You know that wasn't my fault. I didn't kill your son."

"LIAR!"

"Enough!" Rico spat. He set his hands on the sarcophagus' lid. "It's in the past. Everything is in the past . . . including the secrets of immortality."

And he shoved the lid off the coffin.

Chapter 56

THE SARCOPHAGUS' LID CLANGED onto the floor. Rico leaned over the coffin and stared inside. He gasped at what he saw. "It's really here," he said.

I tried to get a better look inside the coffin, but Lynch jerked my hair violently and I whimpered.

"Yes," whispered Zheng. "The Scroll of Everlasting Life. Take it. Seize it for yourself."

Rico reached into the sarcophagus and pulled out a rolled parchment. He held it up and studied its sealed crest—a glob of hardened, red wax with the imprint of a dragon.

"Now open it. Break the seal," Zheng urged.

"Immortality," breathed Rico. He pressed fingers to the seal and snapped it in two.

Immediately, the chamber filled with an unworldly shrieking. The wailing made the hairs on the back of my neck stand on end. It sounded like a hundred souls screaming in chorus. Wind rustled my clothes and swirled throughout the room even though we were deep underground. Brilliant, white light glared from the scroll. Squinting, Rico unrolled the parchment. His face closed in so he could read its ancient script—

A searing blast of energy hit him square in the face, sending him flying into a red pillar. He struck the pillar with the force of a two-ton truck, then tumbled to the ground in a heap. He didn't move. The scroll was still clenched in his fist. Rico groaned, but it came out more as a rasp. His face was mangled as though fire had melted his flesh. Blood pooled beneath him.

I averted my eyes. The sight of Rico's broken form made me feel sick.

Zheng let out a high-pitched cackle. "Fool," he said, pacing closer to Rico's unmoving body. "You are a fool, Mr. Raja."

Rico gasped, gurgling as he struggled to breathe. "You—but you said—"

"What? That you would live forever?" Zheng laughed again. "No, Mr. Raja, there is no immortality here."

"But, there must be—"

"I told you what you wanted to hear. Why would you want to live forever, anyway?"

"No, it's not for me. My daughter—"

"Is going to die, Mr. Raja."

"But she is—*nggh!*—very sick."

"Save your heartbreak. Your daughter will die like everyone else."

At this, Rico looked at his men. "Kill him," he croaked.

But the mercenaries didn't raise their weapons. Lynch chuckled, his breath warm on my cheek and smelling like rotten eggs.

"They do not follow your commands, Mr. Raja." Zheng knelt to seize the scroll in Rico's grasp. "They obey money, and I have made them wealthy men."

"Bastard. Why?"

Zheng moved closer to the sarcophagus. He lowered his voice to a whisper: "For 2,000 years, Qin's followers have attempted to release their emperor from this prison. But we've lacked resources. We infiltrated the Triad in hopes of achieving our goals, but the Chinese government has kept this mound sealed. They even killed grave robbers foolish enough to attempt treasure-seeking raids. Then you come along, the perfect tool, with all your money and guns—" he unrolled the scroll, his expression feral and dangerous, and held it high overhead for all to see "—and you even disarmed the final trap. Thank you, Mr. Raja."

Rico grimaced, clearly in a tremendous amount of pain.

"And now," Zheng's voice rose, swelling like the crescendo of a song, "the Wǔshén spells of our ancestors will be spoken once again. There will be a new China, a new era. And the First Qin Emperor shall rule once more."

Chapter 57

ZHENG READ THE SCROLL ALOUD. He chanted in a language I couldn't understand. Tamora stood aside and watched, a glint of anticipation gleaming in her eyes. Her Glock pistol was still pressed firmly against my father's head. My scalp hurt from Lynch pulling my hair. No amount of struggling would lessen his grip. Nearby, the boys fought to break free from their captors, but they couldn't get away.

Zheng finished reading the scroll.

The chamber grew deathly quiet. Only Rico's gurgling gasps broke the silence.

Then somebody screamed—and it wasn't until later that I realized it was me.

The corpse of Emperor Qin slowly rose from the open sarcophagus. But the corpse didn't climb to its feet like a normal man would do if he was lying down. Instead, the corpse rose as though it were a puppet attached to strings. Qin was nothing but bones. His back was stooped. Strands of thin, white hair clung to his skull. The corpse wore a golden robe, but its edges were frayed and rot pocked its silken cloth.

Qin reminded me of a zombie from a 1980s horror movie. A stench reached my nostrils, threatening to knock me to my knees—a foul combination of the rank stench of urine and the bloated ripeness of a corpse left in the sun. I fought my heaving stomach, fearing that if the smell worsened I'd blow chunks all over Lynch.

On second thought, would that be so bad?

Then, right before my eyes, Emperor Qin metamorphosed into a vibrant man. Skin started forming on his bones, rotten at first, but slowly becoming flesh. His white hair transformed into sleek black hair. Even his deteriorating robe changed to its original state—a rich, flowing garment of shimmering silk. I imagined this must have been how Qin looked just before he died, during the prime years of his life when he conquered the Warring States and united all of China.

Emperor Qin gasped, the first breath since his last.

Zheng knelt in obedience and planted his face against the ground. He spoke foreign words.

Emperor Qin glanced at him and croaked words I couldn't make out. Zheng rose to his feet and offered the emperor a hand. Emperor Qin accepted his help and stepped down from the coffin. Then Qin glided toward the entrance mercenaries had blown into the side of the chamber—his movements unnatural. He didn't appear to be walking, more like he floated across the floor.

Zheng followed. He stopped at the entrance and barked orders at the mercenaries: "Time to earn your coin, men. Tonight we take the city of Xi'an. Tomorrow . . . we take China!"

The mercenaries hooted and hollered. Then they followed Zheng out. Several of them planted explosives just inside the tunnel they'd created. The soldiers holding Jason and Zac captive shoved them down next to Rico. They backed out of the chamber with their guns aimed in case the boys tried to run. Lynch loosened his grip on my hair, and when I turned to kick him in the groin, he shoved me forcefully. My shoulder slammed into the sarcophagus and I fell to the floor.

"Rot and die, little girl. Rot—and—die."

Tamora eased toward the exit, her Glock locked on my father. When she reached the chamber door, she faced us. "How fitting that this chamber will be your tomb, Hank. Considering how you left my son to die in a similar place. At night, I still wake from nightmares of him clawing at stones, fingernails ripping off, as he attempts to escape." She shuddered. "It fills me with great joy knowing you and your children will die just as painfully as he did."

"Tamora—" panted Dad. "Please—I didn't kill your boy!"

"Keep telling yourself that lie," she said, as a mercenary handed her a device with a little red button, "while you spend your final moments in utter darkness, listening to the cries of your children as death takes them one by one."

And she pushed the button.

An explosion sounded. Stone rained down as the tunnel collapsed, sealing us in. We were thrust into darkness . . . locked inside Emperor Qin's burial chamber while Rico wheezed for air.

Part Three

THE TERRACOTTA ARMY

Chapter 58

I HAD NEVER EXPERIENCED SUCH darkness. In the blackness, my hearing seemed heightened. I could hear the painful breaths of Rico, the shallow breathing of my brothers, and something else—a scurrying sound, like the clicking of pincers or the scuttling of spiders on stone.

"Kids, move toward my voice," my father called. "Walk carefully—we don't want to spring a trap in the dark."

"What's that noise?" asked Zac.

"I'm not sure, son. Come closer."

I eased toward his voice, feeling empty air, and my fingers scraped something cold and rough.

White light flared in the darkness. "No need to be blind," said Jason, holding his cell phone high as it cast a soft glow around him.

"Such a resourceful boy," said Dad.

I noticed what my fingers brushed up against— Emperor Qin's sarcophagus. I yanked my hand back and peered inside. The coffin was empty. All that remained were tattered linens and the stench of death. I still couldn't believe what we had just witnessed—a dead man rising from the grave. There was no way Jason could discount the supernatural now, not after seeing that.

"*Nggh!*" Rico groaned painfully. "H-help."

I glanced his way, and although Rico was mostly covered in shadow as he lay slumped against the pillar he'd struck, I could tell he was in dire need of medical attention.

"Please—*nggh*—I think my back is broken."

I went to his side and knelt. "Jason—a little light."

Jason swept his cell phone in my direction, and its light illuminated Rico. His face was gruesome. The blast had mangled his features and part of his nose was missing.

"I'm—sorry—" he wheezed, but he wasn't looking at me. He stared at my father. "Dr. Jones—"

"I'll consider your apology if we make it out of here alive," Dad cut him off.

"I won't be leaving—" Rico grimaced. "Please, I need a favor."

Dad scoffed. "Why should I help you? You threatened to kill my family."

"I have a daughter. Beautiful, just like your Maddie," he coughed, spitting blood, "but she has stage four cancer. Doctors say she has less than a year to live. That's why I sought the Scroll of Everlasting Life—so I could heal her."

Dad stopped inspecting a nearby wall, and glanced at Rico. "I am sorry."

"I failed her." Rico's eyes blurred with tears. "Now she will follow me into the Afterlife."

I cleared my throat as Rico turned his gruesome face to look at me. "My mom died when I was little," I said. "She's been gone for a long time . . . but in a way . . . she never truly left us. Sometimes I feel like she's still around, whispering in my ear, giving me words of encouragement. Death might be a normal part of life, but maybe it's not the end."

Rico smiled weakly.

"We are not meant to live forever," I continued, feeling my confidence brimming the more I spoke. "We are meant to stand aside for the next generation of people so they can have their chance at living."

"You are a strong girl, Maddie Jones," Rico said. "I admire your strength—your wisdom. You remind me of her . . ."

"What is your request?" I asked.

Rico reached into a vest pocket. He pulled out an old-fashioned tape recorder. Was this what Rico spoke into after he repelled down into Pit One with the terracotta warriors?

"This tape recorder is for my daughter," he said, placing it into my hands. "Can you take it to her? Tell her that I love her?"

I touched the compass necklace Mom had given Dad—a symbol of her love. Although I cherished the compass deeply, how wonderful would it have been if she had recorded a message personally to me—a message I could listen to whenever I was down or needed her wisdom? Rico may be about to die, but he had ensured his daughter would hear three powerful words: *I love you.*

"I will," I promised. "What's her name? Where can I find her?"

Rico pointed at the tape recorder. "It's all there, recorded in my words. Thank you, Maddie Jones."

The scurrying noise grew louder. I knew we needed to escape this tomb, but Rico began mumbling, his eyes unfocused in a faraway gaze.

"I'm going ahead of you, sweetheart," he whispered, "to prepare a room for you in heaven." I grasped his hand so he wouldn't be alone—and he exhaled, long and slow, departing this world with his daughter's name gracing his lips one last time . . .

"Amira."

Chapter 59

I WIPED MY EYES ON my sleeve, then touched Rico's eyes and closed them.

"Maddie," Jason said softly. "Are you okay?"

"Yeah," my voice came out hoarse. "Can you put this in your backpack?"

"Sure."

I gave him Rico's tape recorder. He put it away, then I stood and swallowed back tears. We were in a lot of trouble trapped inside Emperor Qin's tomb. I needed to control my emotions if we were going to survive. "How bad is our situation, Dad?"

"It's bad," he said, now searching a nearby terracotta statue to see if its arms were levers that might open a hidden door. "Emperor Qin is going to destroy Xi'an and enslave its populace. He is a powerful and ancient mummy—and there's only one way to stop him."

"General Li Fei and the terracotta warriors?"

"Precisely. I have a feeling the terracotta warriors might have awoken when Zheng read that Wǔshén spell."

Jason groaned. "I can't believe this is happening."

"How do we get out of here?" asked Zac. "Those mercenaries blew up their entrance, and the tunnel we traveled through just leads back to that spiraling slide and a bunch of dead ends."

"The mechanism," said Jason.

"But it's not located here," Dad said, stopping his search to look at us. "It's in the acrobatics pit."

"No, we checked," I said. "It wasn't there—and we believe it's in this room."

"Are you sure?"

I nodded.

The scurrying noise grew louder. It echoed throughout the chamber, sounding like it came from all directions.

"Something is coming," Dad said, motioning to the walls. "Quick—get into the light!"

I hurried to Jason and stood with my back pressed to him, Dad, and Zac. We stared into the darkness just beyond the cell phone light. The noise grew shrill, surrounding us, and I thought I heard something above us. I looked up, but the ceiling was too tall and I could see nothing but shadows overhead.

Zac grabbed my arm, startling me. "Why are the shadows moving?!"

I strained my eyes to stare into the gloom. The shadows seemed to be stirring, moving like water, making their way closer. "I'm not sure—"

Something heavy landed on my shoulder, and I screamed.

Dad was quick. He brushed it off, and I whirled around to find a scorpion the size of a human skull thump against the ground. It quickly got to its feet, then scurried to climb up my leg. I jumped back, screaming again, but Dad stomped on it with a sickening *crack*. Green pus squirted.

"There are hundreds of them," Zac said weakly.

Scorpions with curved tails as sharp as knives swarmed the chamber. Their pincers clacked and clawed, beady eyes gleaming. But they weren't attacking. Instead, they circled us, looking like a black sea made up entirely of deadly arachnids.

"Why are they staying back?" yelled Jason.

"They must be afraid of the light," breathed Dad. "Hold your cell phone high, son."

Jason did as instructed, and the outer edge of our light expanded a bit. The scorpions scurried away from it.

"What'd we do?"

"Search for the mechanism!"

My eyes scoured the dimly lit chamber. Emperor Qin's treasure was heaped in piles, the stone walls arched into a domed ceiling that was shrouded in darkness, terracotta statues stared back like lifeless marionettes, and the golden sarcophagus loomed open and empty. But I saw nothing resembling what we might be searching for.

"What about the map?" Zac suggested.

"No need," Dad said. "The mechanism should be a three-geared device with a lever. It will be obvious."

But it wasn't obvious, at least not to me. Maybe if the four of us moved around the chamber huddled beneath the cell phone's glow we'd see what we were searching for—

Scorpions attacked before I could suggest it.

Three arachnids scurried into the light, pincers snapping. Their sharp tails shot forward, green venom oozing. I jumped out of the way, careful to stay in the light, and kicked the nearest arachnid. The scorpion *crunched* from the force of my blow and went flying into the dark. I turned to stomp on the next one—

But Dad and the boys kicked and punched, knocking scorpions away. Green blood and black exoskeletons lay smashed at their feet.

"Climb into the sarcophagus," Dad instructed.

The four of us clambered into the empty coffin. We stood inside of it, scorpions now scurrying up its sides, but we swatted them away. Now that we stood higher from the floor, Jason's light flooded more of the chamber—and it illuminated the vaulted ceiling overhead. I craned my neck to search, and there! High above Emperor Qin's sarcophagus, I saw a three-geared device with a lever at its center, just like Dad described.

"You've got to be kidding," I grumbled.

The mechanism was at least thirty feet high and unreachable.

Chapter 60

DAD SWORE, AND HIS CUSS word rang in my ears because he rarely used such language. Hey, don't scold me. I realized there were more pressing matters to worry about, but—dang, Dad!

He dropped the F-bomb three more times.

He must have thought our situation hopeless if he used words like that. Dad's panic made me even more scared. I had been waiting for him to come up with an idea or give us directions, but it sounded like he didn't know what to do. The scorpions shrieked and edged closer to the cusp of our cell phone light. Dad swore again, and I tried not to imagine what it would feel like to be impaled by a scorpion's venomous tail or eaten alive.

"If only your mother were here," Dad said. "Her bravery and wits would've saved us."

Wait, I thought. *Would've saved us? Is Dad giving up?!*

"Mom was brave?" asked Jason.

"Oh, yes," said Dad. "She solved countless tomb traps and saved our necks on numerous occasions. I may have book smarts, but she had street smarts. Your mother could solve any puzzle under any circumstance."

I never knew that about Mom. I always assumed she was just a homebody who joined Dad on digs from time to time. But if Mom was brave, did that mean I could be, too?

A massive scorpion scuttled across the sarcophagus—and I kicked it. The arachnid *crunched* under my shoe, shrieking. Green pus sprayed.

Maybe I could.

Killing the creature filled me with confidence. I always wanted to be like Mom. Now I had even more reasons to be like her. I looked around for a way to reach the mechanism. If we climbed atop each other's shoulders we might be able to reach it, but then how would we fight off killer scorpions? Man, what I wouldn't give for a good old-fashioned rock wall right about now.

Wait!

The grooves in the stone walls. They appeared deep enough to grip.

Climbing the walls might work, but glancing at the nearest wall told me I'd have to sprint twenty feet, then climb thirty—all while fighting monstrous scorpions. I'd have to be quick, something I wasn't, and we all know how bad I am at climbing the rock wall in gym class.

A scorpion leapt out of the darkness. I ducked, and it soared over my head and crashed into the sea of arachnids on the other side. Scorpions shrieked, disturbed by the one that struck them—and they clawed, pierced, and stung one another, growing restless. How much longer until the scorpions no longer feared the light? Or worse—what if the phone's battery died?

Okay, Maddie, are you going to let your family die? Or will you be brave like Mom?

The answer was obvious. I just didn't know if I had it in me. Fear made my legs feel heavy like they were glued to the spot. My heart beat painfully fast. Sweat ran down my face, partly from the stifling chamber, but mostly from the stress of our situation. How could I save my family? Heroes saved the day, not me. I was just a fourteen-year-old girl. Maybe if I counted to three I could muster up the courage.

"One," I said, clenching my fists, staring past the scorpions at the section of wall I planned to climb.

"Two."

"Maddie—" I heard Dad faintly say. "What are you doing?"

"No time to explain, Dad," I said. "Three!"

I leapt from the sarcophagus, hit the ground into a roll, then sprang to my feet and ran. The scorpions shrieked— and swarmed. Dad and the boys shouted my name. A scorpion struck with its tail, but I jumped over it completely and kept on running. I was almost to the wall when a horde of arachnids cut me off. I skidded to a stop and turned around. Where was the quickest place to climb?

There!

A section of wall had been exposed when the scorpions moved to attack. It was on the other side of the sarcophagus, barely visible in the dim light. Behind me, I heard scorpions scurrying and their pincers snapping.

"Look out, Maddie!"

Heavy legs clamped onto my arm, pinching through my jacket and into my skin. Without looking, I punched the weight away. The scorpion went flying from my arm and landed atop a dozen more scorpions, screeching. Holy fetch, how close had it been to stinging me?

No time to think like that. Run!

I hurtled a nearby pedestal filled with jewels and sprinted for the wall. I raced past my dad and brothers standing in the open sarcophagus. My actions must have sent the scorpions into a frenzy because now scorpions were scurrying up the coffin's sides. Dad and the boys fought off scorpions, punching and kicking, while Jason's cell phone light bounced all over the room.

I reached the wall and jumped—gripped the grooves and climbed. It was nothing like the rock wall in gym class, with its colorful handholds and easy foot placements. My fingers only fit inside the grooves halfway up to my knuckles. All my weight was held between my fingers and feet—which were scraping the wall, kicking as I ascended. I didn't look down, and the higher I climbed the steeper the wall became as it curved with the vaulted ceiling.

Scorpions raced up the wall after me, but I couldn't let go to defend myself, or else I might fall. Jason must've noticed. His light flashed, following my ascent, and the light knocked scorpions loose before they got close enough to kill.

The chamber grew uncomfortably hot. Poor lighting made it difficult to secure handholds. My fingers cramped and sweat blurred my vision, making the climb even harder. Then the wall suddenly leveled out as it merged with the vaulted ceiling. Six feet loomed between me and the mechanism, but I couldn't climb any farther. Otherwise, I'd be hanging upside down, and there was no way I could hold my weight up then.

Short of breath, I let go with one hand and reached for the lever. My muscles quivered—and my foot slipped. My life flashed before my eyes for the briefest second, then I gripped the wall in both hands and regained my balance. Whoa, I almost plummeted thirty feet to my death.

"Maddie—be careful, sweetie!"

Even in danger Dad still called me *sweetie*. How many times must I tell him not to call me that? At least once more it seemed. "Dad—you know I hate that nickname."

"Sorry, baby girl—*whoa!*—Jason, the light!"

Scorpions approached in a hurry, climbing upside down on the ceiling to reach me. Jason shone his cell phone light, but this time it didn't stop them. They scuttled forward, green venom oozing from their stingers. I realized it was now or never—because if I didn't act now we'd die.

I put all my energy into my legs and jumped.

Chapter 61

I HURTLED WEIGHTLESSLY THROUGH the air. Time seemed to slow. Dad and the boys gasped and scorpions shrieked. The lever was getting closer. My fingers brushed its rough wooden handle. I grasped it, momentum swinging me forward—and the lever suddenly jerked into place.

It worked!

There was a loud *bang*. Clanking gears sounded from inside the walls. Torches sputtered to life throughout the tomb, their green flames ethereal. The ghostly light illuminated the scorpions, and they screeched and hissed as they scurried into cracks in the walls, disappearing from view.

I blew out a breath, still hanging thirty feet in the air. If I never saw another scorpion in my life I'd consider myself blessed.

"Maddie—drop and I'll catch you," Dad called from far below.

I craned my neck to find him. He stood atop the sarcophagus directly beneath me, arms outstretched. I didn't want to let go. Could he catch a fourteen-year-old slick with sweat? But I saw no other way of getting back to the ground, so I swallowed and released the lever.

Wind rushed by, my tummy fluttered, and before I knew it Dad caught me in his arms. He set me down with a tremendous grin. "You truly are your mother's daughter, Maddie."

I smiled, beaming with pride.

Then I heard the lever overhead slide back into its original position. Gears stopped spinning. Bangs and thuds sounded from behind a wall flanked by two terracotta dancers. The statues slowly turned to face one another, their arms upraised to form an arch. Rumbling shook the chamber, and the stone wall between the terracotta dancers eased into the floor. It disappeared completely, revealing a yellowed scroll resting atop a lone pedestal.

The scroll's wax seal was blue and imprinted with links of a chain. Across the room, another wall flanked by terracotta statues rumbled open—and a passageway sloping gently upward appeared. It looked like it might be a way out of the burial chamber.

"Not another scroll," groaned Zac.

"I wonder what this one does?" said Jason.

"It must be the scroll to break chains," my dad said, his voice quivering in anticipation. "And if the scroll does what I think it does, it should free the terracotta warriors from their curse."

Chapter 62

SCROLL IN HAND, WE EXITED the burial chamber. Dad was smart enough to grab a torch on the way out—just in case the scorpions decided to make a second deadly appearance. I hurried along behind him, stumbling now and then on the uneven floor. The stone passageway twisted and turned, rising steadily upward. It took forever, but after what felt like an hour, we came to the foot of some worn stone steps which rose out of sight. We climbed, and I tried to count the number of stairs as we went, but I lost count somewhere around six hundred. Dad's torch spit and crackled, shifting shadows. I watched my feet so I wouldn't stumble in the dark.

We reached the tomb's exit—an already opened set of bronze doors.

"It must've opened when we unlocked the mechanism," said Jason.

Outside, the nighttime air tasted sweet. After hours underground in the stifling confines of a tomb, the cool breeze felt crisp and refreshing. Stars shone brightly overhead, gray clouds scudding across the moon. But on the horizon, a dark thunderstorm brewed. Its ominous clouds were black and red, reminding me of blood.

Lightning flashed, illuminating the city of Xi'an for half a heartbeat. It was hard to tell because of the distance, but it looked like the storm swirled over the city.

"That's unusual," I said.

"What is?" asked Dad.

"The storm over there," I pointed. "I've never seen anything like it."

Dad studied the thunderstorm, his look worrisome. "Legends say that Wŭshén priests of China could rain fire on their enemies from the clouds. Jason—what time is it?"

Jason looked at his watch. "Three in the morning. Why?"

"I'm afraid we don't have much time," Dad said with a heavy sigh. "Let us hurry." And he sprinted toward Pit One where the terracotta warriors were located. The boys and I raced to catch up.

As we entered Pit One, I heard the strangest noises. A din of chains rattled ceaselessly as clangs of metal split the air. Dad moved quickly, and as my feet scampered to keep up, my mouth hung open in astonishment at what I saw.

The terracotta warriors were alive.

Thousands of clay statues were moving, I kid you not. Warriors with cropped beards, mustaches, and goatees tugged at ghostly chains clasped around their ankles. Brown terracotta cracked and flaked as warriors attempted to break free, striking chains with swords, spears, and axes—their blades *clanging* with each hit. But they weren't able to destroy the ethereal chains binding their legs.

Some warriors stopped to stare as we passed. Their sculpted faces were otherworldly, pupil-less eyes unblinking and frightening. I sensed the warriors meant us harm. We were trespassing on sacred ground. We shouldn't be here. I picked up my pace to be closer to Dad.

We passed the chariot and horses. Similar to the warriors, the horses had sprung to life. The bronze animals kicked and stamped, snorted and neighed—but they, too, were chained to the ground.

We found General Li Fei crouched on his knees, meditating. I vaguely remembered him looking like a mighty warrior earlier, sword arm raised. Now his expression was calm behind a sculpted face and beard. His eyes were closed, and since he didn't appear to be breathing, he looked like nothing more than a clay sculpture.

But as we approached his eyes snapped open.

The sight of his eyes startled me. They had no color, no pupils—just the smooth brown of clay. I started to say, "Hey, how's it going?" but Dad stepped in front of me.

The general didn't speak. He simply looked up at my father, his expression unreadable.

Dad bowed. He spoke in Mandarin or some other ancient dialect of Chinese. I knew he was fluent in at least a dozen languages, having learned from years of study overseas. After he finished speaking, he knelt before the general and held out his hands, offering the scroll.

General Li's listless eyes darted to it. Then, very slowly, he reached for the scroll and gripped it in stiff hands. His gaze swept past us to stare at the terracotta army chained in the pit beyond.

"Won't the scroll be booby-trapped?" asked Zac.

"Hush, son," Dad said. "We're about to witness something miraculous."

Chapter 63

GENERAL LI FEI MARCHED TO the front of his army, clenching the scroll in a hardened fist. Clay chipped from his body and crumbled away with each step. As he passed the terracotta warriors, they each turned to bow, showing honor. I still couldn't believe the statues were moving like people. It was an insane sight to behold . . . and kind of cool, too.

General Li stopped before the terracotta army. He bowed.

Bang! All 6,000 warriors snapped to attention.

"Whoa," Jason breathed.

General Li held the scroll high. Then the creepiest thing occurred. The clay covering his mouth cracked open, and a booming voice emerged. His words came out grating like he hadn't spoken in a really long time—because, you know, he hadn't. Standing off to the side, Dad translated the general's words to me and the boys.

"Emperor Qin has been freed from his prison." Warriors shifted restlessly at this, but the general continued undaunted. "He plans to do as he did in life—torment and kill the children of China. Over 2,000 years ago, he forced us to drink a vile potion that turned our souls into eternal clay. He cursed us, keeping our souls from entering the halls of our ancestors. But know this—if we defeat Emperor Qin, our souls might walk amongst our beloveds once more."

The terracotta warriors' clay mouths suddenly ripped open, and they roared. A chill shivered down my spine, giving me goosebumps.

General Li raised a hand for silence. "Aid me, my brothers. Let us rid China of evil. Let us finish what we started 2,000 years ago."

There was a thunderous *stomp*, followed by thousands of warriors shouting, "Fùchóu!" over and over again. It wasn't until later that Dad explained the word meant *revenge*.

General Li snapped the blue wax seal on the scroll. He unrolled the parchment, and when he went to read it, a searing blast of energy struck him square in the face. The clay exterior covering his face exploded away, revealing his real features beneath. They were gruesome and maggoty, with eyes sunken into his skull and leathery skin decayed to the bone—a mummy in every sense of the word.

But the scroll's trap did little to harm the general. I mean, seriously, how could you kill a guy who had already been dead for thousands of years? General Li's lips spread back in a dreadful sneer. A worm slithered through a missing tooth and into his hollowed-out nose. I tried not to vomit as General Li began reciting the scroll's ancient words.

The voice that boomed forth made me shudder. It was bone-rattling and eerie. I covered my ears, trying to dull the noise, but General Li ended the last verse on an S-word that hissed throughout the room like a slithering serpent.

The din of breaking chains rang out.

Terracotta warriors stepped forward, free at last. The clay mummifying their bodies cracked and crumbled as they shook free of the ethereal chains, but their terracotta bodies remained intact. The clay soldiers stood before us ready for battle.

General Li hissed a final word—and just like Emperor Qin, his vitality slowly returned. The hardened clay covering his body crumbled away, and General Li morphed from a mummy into a healthy man. His rotten flesh became healthy and pink. Black hair grew from his skull, a dark sheen to it, and the hard edges of his sculpted face softened. He unsheathed his sword—now a vibrant warrior—and the terracotta army banged their swords, spears, and axes.

"Fùchóu!" they shouted their war cry all together.

Afterward, I leaned in close and slapped the general on the shoulder. "Atta boy," I said. "So what's next, big guy?"

General Li glared at me and growled.

I forced a laugh, then Jason yanked me aside so I wouldn't become Li's first kill. "Don't mind her," he said. "She's a little slow." Then he mouthed to me, "What's wrong with you?"

"Hey, I'm sorry," I said. "How was I supposed to know the guy has the sense of humor of a dead man?"

Chapter 64

THE NEXT THING I KNEW, I was riding alongside General Li Fei in his war chariot. Four bronze horses pulled us forward at a gallop, and I held on tightly as we rumbled down the road. Behind me, Dad and the boys rode with the cavalry—a hundred terracotta soldiers mounted on horses, armed with crossbows and swords. Dad had been given an axe and a bronze horse, while Jason wore a sheathed sword on his hip and Zac gripped a crossbow with a quiver of bolts slung across his shoulder. My brothers rode a single horse together, Zac on the back. Meanwhile, I gripped an eight-foot spear with a bronze-bladed tip.

And did I mention we now wore armor and junk? I'm talking bronze breastplates, gauntlets, and helmets.

Yeah, the Jones family was riding for war.

The infantry came after us—thousands of warriors marching shoulder to shoulder, rank after rank. The terracotta army marched toward Xi'an, which loomed miles ahead. The thunderstorm had brewed into a monstrous hurricane ready to devour the city.

Nearly an hour later, the terracotta army marched through the streets of Xi'an with me and the general leading the way. General Li seemed to be steering us closer to a towering skyscraper with at least fifty floors, beige concrete walls, and blue glass windows.

"It's the Shaanxi Information Mansion," Jason shouted from behind. "The tallest building in all of Xi'an."

High above the skyscraper, the eye of the storm swirled—making it appear like whatever caused the unnatural weather might be positioned atop the building. I shuddered, imagining Emperor Qin using otherworldly powers to rain fire from the clouds.

Not many people roamed the streets this late at night. The few bystanders we did pass stared with wide eyes and open mouths at the terracotta army. Some clambered to get out of the way. Occasionally, parked vehicles blocked our path, but General Li's warriors stepped forward and cleared cars from the road with inhuman strength.

At one point, an entire apartment building awoke to watch us pass. They poured into the street to see General Li in his ancient Chinese regalia, and to gawk at the American family riding alongside him. They held cell phones and recorded the terracotta army as we marched by.

"Nothing to see here," Zac shouted at the onlookers. "We're just your typical army come back from the dead to defeat the soul of China's first emperor. Move along."

I palmed my face. Oh, brother!

Chapter 65

THE TERRACOTTA ARMY HALTED in front of the Shaanxi Information Mansion. The skyscraper loomed above us, its topmost floor engulfed in the swirling vortex of the storm. Fierce winds whipped about, snapping the purple tips of my hair as it stuck out beneath the bronze helmet. The horses snorted and stamped—almost as though they anticipated the battle to come.

As the army halted, more than a dozen mercenaries rushed from the skyscraper's entrance to block the glass doors leading inside. They shouldered automatic assault rifles and aimed them at the terracotta army. Zheng walked out last. He glared at General Li, then pointed his tattooed hand at me.

"How'd you escape the tomb?" he snarled. "We sealed it shut."

"Meh," I shrugged. "I guess you forgot you're dealing with Maddie Jones."

General Li raised a fist.

Immediately, the infantry rushed forward and formed lines for an attack. Behind me, the cavalry and crossbowmen awaited the general's command. Although the mercenaries wore Kevlar bullet-proof plating and gripped automatic assault rifles, they appeared nervous—shifting restlessly, guns jumping from target to target. I couldn't blame them. I'd be nervous if 6,000 undead warriors stood opposed to me, too.

To be honest, I *was* nervous. My hands trembled. The spear gripped in my hand felt clammy with sweat. Butterflies fluttered in my stomach. Nah, forget butterflies. It was more like gigantic-winged dragons zoomed around. I'd never been in a battle before, excluding countless hours playing video games. But those were fake—this was real. Perhaps we should've stayed put at the Museum of Terracotta Warriors.

Lightning flashed, followed by the immediate *crack* of thunder. It began sprinkling.

Zheng yelled out orders. Mercenaries darted into motion, preparing to bar our path into the building.

I gulped. The battle for Xi'an was about to begin.

Chapter 66

GUNSHOTS RANG OUT AND I flinched. Mercenaries fired automatic rifles into the terracotta warriors. Bullets hit their mark, but bodies didn't drop to the ground. I mean, come on, how do you kill something that's made entirely of clay?

General Li shouted a command.

Crossbowmen aimed, fired.

Twang! Bowstrings snapped. Hundreds of bolts soared overhead, then rained down onto the mercenaries.

Mercenaries ducked for cover. A majority of the bolts struck nothing more than concrete, but a few hit their targets—striking chests, backs, and arms. But they were deflected by the mercenaries' Kevlar plating. I recalled Detective Murphy shooting at a soldier after the car crash, and how bullets couldn't hurt her. It appeared crossbow bolts wouldn't work here, either.

Twang! A solitary bolt flew.

"So that's how the weapon works," I heard Zac say.

"Wicked," said Jason.

Goodness, you couldn't take those boys anywhere.

Zac's bolt struck the ground near Zheng's feet. It outraged him. "Kill!" he yelled at his men. *"Kill them all!"*

The mercenaries fired more rounds into the throng of terracotta warriors. I dropped down behind General Li's chariot and covered my head. Standing beside me, Li unsheathed his sword. Bullets walloped him, but he didn't seem to feel a thing. He raised his sword overhead, then swiped it down, pointing the way forward.

The infantry charged, shouting their war cry: "Fùchóu!"

Guns stopped firing momentarily. I peeked over the edge of the chariot. Mercenaries scrambled up the skyscraper's steps, fleeing for cover. Several resumed firing their guns after reloading, striking terracotta infantrymen rushing to kill. But the clay soldiers ran on, invincible.

"Shōufèi!" the general bellowed a command at his cavalry.

Mounted soldiers pulled swords from their scabbards, and yelled. Bronze horses spurred into a gallop, armor flashed by, and before I realized it, Dad and the boys were riding headlong into battle screaming at the top of their lungs.

Holy fetch, this was nuts!

Fearing for their safety, and encouraged by their bravery, I stood and squeezed my spear tightly. General Li yanked the reins of his horses, and the war chariot lurched forward. Its wheels rumbled across the concrete. The terracotta army drowned the mercenaries in their tidal wave onslaught, and I realized our superior numbers were winning.

Then a fiery meteor roared across the sky. It broke through blood-red clouds, black smoke trailing behind it, and it crashed into the charging cavalry . . .

Chapter 67

HORSES AND WARRIORS EXPLODED into the air. Flame and smoke mushroomed like a miniature atomic bomb. The ground shook violently and a thunderous boom sounded. The horses pulling General Li's chariot whinnied and bucked—and the chariot tumbled over and fell to the ground. I went sprawling onto concrete, scraping my hands and bruising my knees.

Blinded by chaos, rain, and flying debris—I couldn't see my family. What happened to Dad and the boys? My heart climbed to my throat, feeling like it might burst. They rode with the cavalry. What if they were killed in the blast?

I scrambled to my feet, gritted my teeth against the pain, and ran toward the destruction. I didn't wait to see if General Li followed. Unmoving terracotta warriors littered the ground. Fires raged here and there. Large slabs of concrete rubble were scattered all over the place, steel wires protruding at twisted angles. My head was spinning, but I shouted until my voice was hoarse.

"Dad! Jason! Zac! Answer me!"

Somebody groaned a few feet away. I rushed toward their voice. A terracotta warrior was pinned beneath a huge block of concrete rubble. I attempted to help him, but the warrior set his hands beneath the debris and lifted the concrete off his chest—all three tons of it. Geez! These guys were undead supermen. All around, warriors impacted by the meteor blast slowly climbed to their feet.

But I still couldn't find my boys.

Smoke burned my eyes, making me cough. I looked up. Lightning flashed—and I thought I saw a solitary figure in a golden robe standing atop the skyscraper, arms upraised toward the ominous clouds. Thunder boomed. The flash of light faded and I lost sight of the figure—

—just as another meteor roared across the sky. It rained from the clouds, but the meteor didn't plummet toward the terracotta army—it catapulted right into the heart of the city.

Explosions.

Fire.

Even more destruction.

Then a meteor shower rained down from the heavens. Nearly a dozen meteors blasted into the city. Emperor Qin must be summoning them with dark magic, enveloping the buildings and streets in ruin and brimstone. I whirled around to find General Li—the only person who might be able to stop Emperor Qin—but he wasn't in sight. Where did he go?

"Dad! Boys! Can you hear me?!"

Maybe I'd find my family among those battling on the frontlines. Disoriented from the smoke and rain, I ran with my spear and charged through a group of terracotta warriors reorganizing themselves into ranks. I bounded over a concrete block and emerged near the steps leading up to the skyscraper. The battle here had become a leaderless riot. Mercenaries fired guns into terracotta warriors, and the warriors fought with swords, spears, and axes. As I scanned the combatants, I saw a mercenary become overwhelmed by a dozen warriors, and he went down flailing and screaming.

"None may enter here! Keep back!"

I glanced up the steps and saw Zheng armed with a sword. He stood before General Li, blocking him from entering the building. General Li's dark cloak billowed out like great wings. The general took a step forward, and Zheng swung his blade. It arced in for a killing blow, but with a flick of his wrist, General Li deflected the strike. Crimson energy flared where their swords kissed.

Zheng went flying twenty feet into the air. He slammed into the skyscraper's beige walls, then tumbled down its steps. General Li disappeared inside the building.

Dad and the boys were still missing, but if the general couldn't get to the rooftop then he wouldn't be able to stop Emperor Qin. I suddenly found myself facing a difficult decision: Did I go after General Li? Or did I search the battlefield for my missing family?

My emotions screamed to find Dad and the boys. But if I did that, then more meteors would strike the city, killing people. Why was the choice so difficult? My heart and mind battled one another to decide.

Then I surprised even myself as my feet raced toward the skyscraper's entrance. I'd made my choice—I would make sure General Li reached Emperor Qin. After that, well, I would rush back downstairs and find my family. It wasn't my first choice, but it was a rational one—and one that might lessen the loss of life for the people of Xi'an.

I raced up the stairs leading to the skyscraper's entrance two at a time. I reached the glass doors leading inside. I grasped a metal handle and tugged—but something heavy slammed into my side. My feet lifted from the ground. I struck the ground hard—my head smacking concrete. Stars flashed before my eyes as white, hot pain lanced through my head.

Dazed, I glanced up to see that a mercenary had tackled me.

"You're not getting away," Lynch breathed in my ear, stinking of sweat and blood. "Not this time, little girl."

Chapter 68

LYNCH GRABBED MY SPEAR AND flung it away. I fought to break free, but he gripped my hair and tugged. Sharp pain shot through my scalp. He held me so our faces were a foot apart, his sour breath wafting beneath my nose.

Lynch unsheathed a combat Army knife and pressed its cold steel against my cheek. "You gave me this," he growled, tapping his eyepatch with the blade's sharp tip. "Your father did this . . ." his other eye was bloodshot. "Do you have any idea how painful it is to be punched in the eye? Twice? Hmmm?"

I squirmed, raking at the hand gripping my hair. The toes of my shoes scraped the rain-soaked ground.

A nasty grin stretched across Lynch's pale, cracked lips. "You have such pretty eyes. No one should have such pretty eyes." He traced the blade's sharp edge against my cheek— and it cut, stinging. Warm blood trickled down my chin. I tried not to make a sound, not wanting to give Lynch the satisfaction, but I couldn't help it. I whimpered.

He grinned again.

"Big, dumb jerk—lemme go!" I screamed.

I kicked and punched, but none of my efforts mattered since he was so heavily armored in combat gear. Plus, Lynch was a grown-up—a muscular one at that. He cackled, positioning the tip of his knife near my eye. I shut them tight, trying to turn away, but he kept my face staring forward.

"Let's remove those pretty—*agghh!*"

Something wet splattered my face—and it wasn't the rain. Lynch cried out in pain, dropping me. I hit the ground, and when I opened my eyes, I saw that one of Lynch's hands had been pierced by a crossbow bolt.

"Son of a—" he cursed, holding the wounded hand.

Lightning flashed. Rain hammered.

For half a heartbeat, I saw Zac standing thirty feet away aiming a crossbow. He wore a mercenary's night-vision goggles. Jason stood beside him, sword in hand. They were covered in black ash and soot, hair sopping wet.

My brothers were alive!

Then lightning darkened and I couldn't see them anymore.

Lynch turned his glare on me, and I scrambled to my spear and picked it up. I whirled around, twirling its wooden shaft—but Lynch was there, crouching low in a knife-fighting stance.

"So be it, girl," he growled. "Let's do this. Come on—come on—*kill me!*"

I jabbed.

He sidestepped and moved in close. Slashed. The edge of his knife scraped my bronze breastplate—it protected me.

I leapt rearward, putting some distance between us. I couldn't afford another mistake like that. Although I had the superior weapon and was outfitted in armor, Lynch was a skilled fighter. If he got in close he'd finish me off.

Keep him back, I told myself.

Lynch circled, his good eye scanning for an opening. Another crossbow bolt came soaring through the rain, but it struck Lynch's Kevlar plating and bounced away. He chuckled—and feigned an attack.

I flinched—then jabbed, jabbed, swiped, and jabbed.

But Lynch was fast, blazing fast, as quick as anyone I'd ever seen. He deflected each of my spear attacks with his combat knife. And when I struck him with the spear's shaft, he absorbed the blow against his arm. He reached in and cut, this time nicking my exposed arm, drawing blood. I hissed and jumped backward to get away.

"Don't you just love a good knife fight?"

"Shut up!" I yelled, heart racing.

What should I do? How could I win? Lynch was toying with me. I needed to think.

But he attacked before I could plan my next move—stab, slash, and punch. His knife work missed, but the punch grazed my head. I stumbled to the side, vision blurring. Another bolt hurtled through the air, missing. Zac probably didn't want to shoot Lynch directly, afraid he might hit me instead. A deflected bolt could ricochet and strike me by mistake.

I shook off the blow, and now I was on the attack, driving Lynch back on his heels. Lynch darted rearward and parried my jabs with his blade—occasionally dodging or ducking or rolling aside. I stayed with him like a quick lioness chasing her prey.

A punch was thrown and I ducked beneath the blow. When I refocused on Lynch, I saw his scarred face worked up in a sneer. I guess he thought he could finish me off quickly.

But you messed with the wrong girl.

Lynch slashed and I rolled. I came up squeezing my spear in slippery hands. Everything was so wet from the rain I feared I'd drop my weapon. Then I saw it—an exposed soft spot in Lynch's combat gear, a weakness. It was beneath his arm, a rip in the Kevlar's fabric, exposing his bare skin like a chink in knight's armor. If I could just get a clean shot . . .

Lynch charged and slashed, stabbed and punched.

I deflected his blade with my spear, then dove out of the way. He kept pressing forward, though, so I swung wildly with my spear. A lucky slash struck his knuckles, making him drop the blade.

"Damn you!" he swore. "That's it, I'm done playing games." Lynch grabbed the holstered pistol strapped to his waist, a gun so big it looked like a hand cannon, and he pointed it right at me.

I stopped dead in my tracks, breathing deeply. Aiming his gun, Lynch's weakness was exposed. But if I made any sudden movements, he'd shoot me dead. I needed a distraction, something to make him look away for a split second.

One of Zac's bolts soared from the darkness and hit Lynch in the leg. It didn't hurt the giant mercenary, but he glanced at the bolt as it ricocheted away—long enough to cause the distraction I needed. I threw my spear.

It spiraled through the air.

Lynch looked up—just as the spear's bronze blade pierced him in the ribs. He cried out in pain, dropping the gun, and I ran up and kicked it. The weapon skidded out of reach. Lynch fell to his knees, gripping the spear sticking out of his side.

"Curse—you—" he struggled to say. "Aghh!" Blood squirted as he attempted to pull out the spear.

"I wouldn't do that if I were you," I said. "The spear might've nicked a vital artery, and if it did, you'll bleed out in seconds."

He let go of the spear, panting. "*Nghh*—I swear, girl— if I survive this, you'll pay."

The boys came rushing up. Jason grinned from ear to ear. "Maddie—that was so—"

"Insane. Cool. Amazing," Zac finished.

"Yeah, what he said."

I smiled, glad to see my brothers alive. "Wait, where's Dad?"

"His horse fell on top of him when the meteor exploded," Jason said.

"He might've broken his leg," Zac put in.

"But he's alive. He sent us to find you."

Howling winds made me look up. Overhead, the storm seemed to be swirling faster, gathering strength. I was willing to bet that if General Li couldn't defeat Emperor Qin, we'd all be dead within the next twenty-four hours.

"Tell Dad I'm okay," I said. "I'm gonna help General Li reach the skyscraper's rooftop."

"No way—we're coming with you," Zac said.

Jason nodded.

Man, I loved my brothers. They wouldn't back down from a fight no matter what.

Lynch groaned. "I mean it, little girl—*nghh!*—you'll be hearing from me again."

"Maybe," I said, glancing at his wound. "But not today." Then I turned and rushed for the skyscraper's entrance, the boys jogging behind me. God, I hoped we weren't too late.

Chapter 69

INSIDE THE SKYSCRAPER'S MAIN lobby, we found mercenaries' unconscious bodies sprawled across the marble floor. Deep sword gouges were cut into the marble. Bullet holes peppered the walls. It appeared there had been a spectacular battle here moments earlier.

The victor stood amidst the downed mercenaries, sword held in one hand, sheath in the other. General Li looked like a mighty Chinese warrior with his cloak fluttering from winds wafting inside the open door. Heck, as commander of the terracotta army, he must have had powers the other warriors didn't. But all those images faded when I realized why General Li hadn't gone up to the rooftop yet.

He didn't know how to work the elevator.

"Do you need help, big guy?" I asked, approaching the general cautiously from behind.

General Li sheathed his sword and growled.

I shook my head. "We seriously need to work on your people skills, dude. Come on—over here—" And I led him to the elevator doors and pressed a button with an arrow pointing UP. We waited for the elevator to arrive.

"Stop!" someone shouted.

I turned to see Zheng, the man with the tattooed hand, stumble inside the main lobby. He was limping and using the wall to support his weight. An arm was draped across his wounded body. His free hand gripped a sword.

"Stop," Zheng panted. "I can't let you interrupt Emperor Qin's spell."

"Not this guy again," groaned Zac.

"Seriously," said Jason. "Bro needs to know when to throw in the towel."

The elevator doors chimed, then opened. General Li stepped inside, waiting. He didn't know what to do next.

"Guys—I gotta go!" I said.

"Then go." Jason brandished his sword. "We'll take care of this twerp."

"Are you sure you can handle Zheng?"

Zac shouldered his crossbow, night vision goggles resting casually on top of his head. "I think you've forgotten something, Maddie."

"What?" I asked.

"We kick ass, too."

I smiled—then I rushed inside the elevator and pressed a button for the top floor. The elevator doors started to close, but right before they shut completely, I got one last glimpse of my brothers in their ancient bronze armor as they faced off against the man with the tattooed hand, preparing to do battle.

Cheesy elevator music played softly. The song sounded like an orchestrated version of a popular pop song, but I couldn't identify which song it was. A bell chimed every time we passed a floor. General Li brooded beside me, not saying a word. Not that we could understand each other, but some conversation was better than no conversation.

"So," I finally spoke. "How have you been?"

General Li sniffled. He busied himself with his sword, which suddenly needed sharpening.

"Well," I said. "This isn't awkward at all."

Chapter 70

ON THE ROOFTOP, WINDS whipped about, threatening to knock me off. Rain sheeted sideways, and it was so cold it felt like buckets of ice water emptied repeatedly over my head. The lighting was poor. The only illumination came from a single flood light that hung over a door leading back inside. It cast long, menacing shadows across silvery pipes, air conditioning equipment, and steel scaffolding used by workers to wash the building's windows. Head bent and eyes narrowed against the downpour, I followed General Li as he approached a golden figure standing on the edge of the skyscraper.

Emperor Qin.

The emperor's back was to us as he stared out at the city of Xi'an. His golden robe snapped like flags atop a battlement, and his arms were raised to the blood-red clouds. The eye of the storm swirled directly over him as streaks of red lightning shot down from the sky. Thunder rent the air.

As we approached, I realized Emperor Qin was chanting in a strange language. His voice hissed like a serpent oozing venom—

—and a meteor suddenly shot through the clouds and blasted toward the city. It struck a building several miles away. An explosion flared up.

I gulped. We had to stop him.

General Li stepped in front of me, sword drawn. "Qín Shǐ Huáng!" he boomed.

Emperor Qin lowered his hands and turned around. When his glowing eyes met Li's, he revealed a curved sword hidden inside his robe. "Lǐ Jiāngjūn," he hissed.

They began speaking in harsh tones. I couldn't understand what was being said, but it seemed that thousands of years had done little to quench the hatred they felt for one another. I began to retreat, realizing I'd done my part to ensure this meeting took place, but before I could take two steps back—Emperor Qin lunged.

One second, he stood near the rooftop's edge, and the next, he wasn't. It was as if he had moved too quickly for the naked eye to see. Emperor Qin materialized before the general, curved sword slashing—but General Li darted into motion just as fast.

The two ancient warriors clashed in mid-air, sword to sword.

Lightning streaked across the sky. Thunder rumbled. Crimson and gold energy flared from their strike, engulfing both warriors in unnatural power that ebbed and churned, swirling around them.

Swords touching, the emperor and general spat curses in each other's face—then General Li pressed the attack. He swiped a series of quick slashes. Qin blocked each strike, and on the last hit, colorful energy flared and a shockwave surged. The impact of their blades sent rainwater flying out in all directions, and the force hit me like a category five hurricane. Wind struck me in the chest, knocking me off my feet. I landed on my back and my breath left me in a *whoosh*.

Gasping for air, I saw General Li's next sword strike miss—and his sharpened blade cut right through a steel pipe. Holy fetch, these guys fought like titans.

But one good thing had occurred while they battled.

Emperor Qin no longer rained meteors down onto the city.

Soaked from the rain even through my bronze armor, I crawled to the rooftop's edge so I wouldn't become collateral damage. I was in over my head in this fight. The ancient warriors fought with supernatural elements that could kill me in a flash. I needed somewhere to hide, so I found an air conditioning unit and ducked down behind it. Now out of the way, I peeked around its corner to see the epic brawl unfold . . .

But something cold and hard pressed against the back of my head. A gun cocked. "Well, well, well, if it isn't Maddie Jones," hissed Tamora Rose, her British accent sending my nerves into shock. "I'm going to enjoy killing you."

Chapter 71

I TURNED AROUND SLOWLY, hands held up. Tamora was dripping wet from the rain. Smeared mascara ran down her cheeks, making her appear nightmarish. Her Glock pistol was aimed directly at my face.

"How'd you escape the tomb?" she asked.

I swallowed.

"Answer me!"

"I pulled a secret lever."

"Of course," she breathed. "Tombs and their blasted hidden passageways. Where is your father?"

I pointed.

"Down below? And your brothers?"

"Same. Tamora—why are you doing this? I thought you were my friend."

"Friend?" Her face twisted into a dreadful sneer. "I'm not your friend, love. Never have been. Not since that horrible day with your father in South America."

"South America?" I repeated, trying to search my memory. "Wasn't that, like, ten years ago?"

"Ten long years," Tamora breathed. "You were only four at the time, but my son Martin was nineteen. He joined me and your father on a dig in Ecuador. We sought an Inca mummy king—Atahualpa. We found a tomb believed to be his, so Hank and Martin excavated the site. But the place was booby-trapped, and when poisonous darts fired from the walls and struck them, Hank revealed his true colors. He ran like a coward and left my son to die."

"My dad would never do that," I protested.

"You don't know your father like I do, Maddie. He's a selfish bastard who cares only for himself. He should've died in that tomb—not my son."

An explosion sounded behind me. I flinched and glanced toward the noise. The battle between Emperor Qin and General Li continued waging. Their swords clashed and energy swirled from the thunderous strike. Distantly, I heard the faint sounds of sirens, most likely from ambulances and fire trucks as they sped through the city toward the flames of destruction caused by the meteors. I brought my focus back to Tamora.

"Why awaken the soul of an ancient mummy?" I asked. "He's destroying the city!"

Tamora adjusted the grip on her pistol. "It's all for history, love. Once Emperor Qin regains control of China, I'll have access to countless dig sites—places archaeologists never dreamed existed. Killing your family was simply icing on the cake."

"You won't get away with it," I said. "General Li will win."

Tamora threw her head back and laughed. "You think you're so clever, Maddie Jones. Truth is—you wouldn't have reached China if it weren't for me." She must have noticed my puzzled expression, because she added, "The shipment of mummies—I authorized your travel knowing you kids hid inside the crate. And you know what? That's not even the best part. Brace yourself, love, because here's the sweetest nugget . . .

"I killed your mother."

"What?" I stammered.

"I poisoned her while she was in labor with Zac."

"No—she died in childbirth."

Tamora laughed again. "She died because I switched her IV bag with frog poison, the same poison my son was inflicted with in that God-forsaken tomb."

"You—killed—her?"

"Oh, say it again—it sounds even better coming from you."

"Aaaarrrgh!" I let out a throaty scream and flung myself at Tamora, tackling her to the ground. Her gun went off . . .

Chapter 72

BANG!

The bullet ricocheted off the ground and struck an air vent. My heart jolted into hyperdrive, beating painfully fast, and I grabbed her gun hand before she could fire again. We wrestled for the weapon, rolling, twisting, and kicking. Rain hammered. Lightning flashed. Meanwhile, Emperor Qin and General Li fought sword to sword, with the fate of China hanging in the balance.

I had forgotten about everything. I'd forgotten that I was short and skinny and fourteen, whereas Tamora was a tall, full-grown woman. All I knew was that I wanted to hurt her badly and I didn't care how much I got hurt in return. Perhaps it was the shock of learning about my mother's murder, but the revelation fueled my punches, kicks, and jabs.

"Let—go!" roared Tamora, punching me in the face with her free hand.

I reeled from the blow, but I didn't release my grip on her gun. "NEVER! YOU KILLED MY MOM!"

Three more rounds went off, but they all fired wildly into the night.

Tamora's knee struck me in the stomach. I doubled over, gasping. But I didn't let go of her Glock, fearing I'd be shot if I did. My survival depended on gripping the gun with all of my strength—there was no letting go.

So I head-butted her instead.

Crack! Our heads smacked together. White hot pain lanced through my forehead. Tamora's eyebrow split. Blood sprayed. She screamed, letting go of the gun—but I dropped it, too. The rain made it slippery. The weapon skidded across wet ground and stopped just on the skyscraper's edge.

Tamora and I froze. We both stared at the weapon. Then she let out a throaty yell and bounded for it. I grunted and dove. We touched its handle at the same time— knocking the weapon from our grasp. The Glock skidded over the skyscraper's edge and plummeted hundreds of feet to the courtyard below.

Tamora roared, and before I could get my hands up, she grabbed my neck and squeezed. Fingers tightened. Her nails dug into my skin, stinging. I tried to inhale a large gulp of air, but I choked. She was cutting off my circulation—I couldn't breathe!

Tamora's eyes were wild, made even more demonic by her smeared make-up. "Time to die, Maddie—" she growled, biting her lip as she put all of her strength into squeezing my neck.

My eyes bulged. My neck was on fire. I punched and punched, but Tamora accepted the blows, not bothering to defend herself. A sudden fear struck me—this was it. This was how I died.

Then I remembered my second go-to move. If you can't kick them in the junk—jab them in the eye. So I poked Tamora with two fingers, hard.

"Arggh!" She reeled from the blow, clutching her face.

I rolled over, gasping. Sweet air filled my lungs, but it hurt to breathe. My throat burned. I climbed to my feet and looked around. Tamora was rubbing her eyes. She wasn't paying attention to me. I glanced around for something to fight her with, but I didn't see anything useful.

Looks like we're brawling.

I lunged. My fist arced in for a strong right hook, aimed at her jaw. But Tamora opened her bloodshot eyes and ducked. My punch missed. Momentum made me keep charging past—and I felt her boot ram into my back.

Screaming, I went over the skyscraper's edge.

Chapter 73

I TWISTED IN MID-AIR, GRASPING and clawing for something—anything—to stop my fall from the skyscraper. My fingers brushed the ledge. I squeezed with every ounce of energy I could muster. My fingers gripped it tight—and my body swung into the rigid skyscraper wall.

"Argh!" I grunted in pain as I heard a loud pop. It felt like my arm had been pulled out of socket.

Gasping, I looked down. Empty air and seven hundred feet loomed beneath me. Chill rain and wind hammered. My fingers throbbed. Above, I heard thunderous clangs from Emperor Qin's and General Li's swords as they fought. Flashes of red and gold energy sparked into the night, flashing from the top of the skyscraper and illuminating the blood-red clouds high above.

Then Tamora appeared. She glowered down at me.

"Your father was supposed to watch you die," she said, her voice barely audible over the wind. "But I guess this will suffice. If I'm lucky, Hank will see you fall and feel the same helplessness I felt when Martin was taken from me."

"Tamora—*NO!*" I shouted, struggling to get a better grip.

"Goodbye, Maddie Jones."

She stepped on my fingers with her boot, digging in her heel. My fingers *popped* and I screamed. Tamora's malevolent grin widened. My grip started to give way . . .

BOOOM! A deafening explosion of light blasted into the sky.

Tamora whirled around—just as a body slammed into her. It looked like Emperor Qin. His golden robe fluttered as he and Tamora went flying from the rooftop in a tangle of arms and legs. I craned my neck to watch them fall, and I glimpsed a sword stabbed into Emperor Qin's heart. It looked like General Li's blade. Tamora screamed and flailed as they fell one hundred feet, two hundred feet—the concrete courtyard fast approaching.

Emperor Qin's golden robe flapped wildly. Tamora flailed desperately—and right when they were about to strike the ground—a shockwave of golden light surged. It glowed like the force of a small sun. I shut my eyes to block its stinging glare. When the light died away, I opened my eyes expecting to see Emperor Qin's and Tamora's broken bodies strewn across the ground. Instead . . .

Look, this is going to sound crazy, but where their broken bodies should have been, there was nothing but an impact zone of scorched asphalt. No bodies. No Emperor Qin. No Tamora Rose. Just scorch marks and a lot of terracotta warriors moving closer to inspect.

"Where'd they go?" I breathed.

My fingers ached from being stepped on. Grunting, I turned my attention back to the ledge. I attempted to pull myself up, but I didn't have the strength. General Li approached the rooftop's edge. His cloak billowed fiercely from the hard rain and wind. He glanced down. I couldn't tell if he was staring at me or at where his vanquished foe should've been. He didn't look happy.

"Hey, a little help!" I said, dangling right beneath his feet.

General Li made eye contact, and scowled. It seemed like he was about to turn around, to leave me hanging, but he crouched and offered his hand.

Chapter 74

I RODE THE ELEVATOR BACK down with General Li. The brooding silence was just as awkward as it had been going up. We reached the main lobby, and General Li led me to my family where I was reunited with them amidst the debris and ruin of the Shaanxi Information Mansion. Dad sat on a busted slab of concrete as he tended his wounded leg. Thankfully, his leg wasn't broken, but he had sprained it when the bronze horse fell on top of him. A purple bruise could be seen on his thigh through his ripped pants leg.

Jason and Zac stood over Zheng. The gangster's eyes were swollen from a blow to the head. One of his legs seeped blood from a crossbow bolt that was still pierced in his thigh. Zheng looked like he had just stepped out of a boxing ring after fighting two heavy-weight champions. A terracotta warrior gripped his tattooed hand tightly, which told me he was being held prisoner.

I looked at my brothers. They both seemed to hold their chins a little higher, chests puffed out.

Oh, brother!

But I was proud of them. And thankful they hadn't been hurt.

"How'd you guys beat him?" I asked.

"With this baby." Zac showed me his crossbow. "I shot him in the leg."

"And I pummeled him with my sword." Jason thumped the hilt of his sheathed blade.

"Wow, you guys are like heroes or something," I said.

They both beamed.

I sat beside Dad on the busted slab of concrete. "Are you okay?"

"It's hard to walk," he said, grimacing. "But I'll be fine. How about you?"

I felt miserable and extremely tired. The cut on my arm needed medical attention. My shoulder was out of socket, not to mention my fingers throbbed from being stepped on. A couple of them were likely broken. But none of that mattered at the moment.

"Dad, I need to know something. Tamora said—"

He put a hand up. "She didn't tell you everything, Maddie."

"But she said you killed her son."

"It's true, I'm partly to blame for Martin's death." There was a hint of sadness in his voice. "But I didn't kill him."

"What happened?"

He closed his eyes and sighed deeply. "A booby-trap went off as we excavated a tomb. Martin was struck by a poisonous dart. The poison made him weak. I tried to carry him out—but a tribe of local Indians ambushed us. They were guarding the sarcophagus of King Atahualpa.

"We fled deeper inside the tomb and hid from our attackers, but Martin needed medical attention. So I made the difficult decision to leave him and seek help. When I returned with Tamora and the others, he had . . . he wasn't . . ." a sob escaped Dad's lips.

"And you told Tamora all of this?"

"God, yes, a thousand times. After all these years, I thought she had finally accepted the truth."

The truth, I thought. Dad didn't know half of it. He didn't know Tamora had held a grudge against our family for nearly a decade. Or that she killed the most important woman in our lives.

"Um, Dad, there's something I need to tell you."

"What is it, Maddie?"

"It's about Mom—"

A commotion broke out behind me, interrupting our conversation. I turned to see Zheng struggling to break free as General Li stood menacingly over him. Zheng spat at the general's feet, then began speaking in harsh tones. He growled something in Mandarin or some ancient dialect of Chinese.

"What's he saying?" I asked Dad.

"He demands to know what happened to Emperor Qin," Dad answered. "He wants to know why the emperor disappeared in a flash of golden light."

General Li spoke, and I listened to Dad as he translated. "I slew the emperor," he said. "The light was his body returning to his tomb. Emperor Qin's soul is finished—damned for all eternity. He shall never rise again."

Zheng slumped. His dreams for a new China were shattered.

I scooted off the slab of busted concrete and approached the general. "What about Tamora? I asked.

"What happened to the woman who fell with Emperor Qin?"

General Li studied me.

"Dad—can you translate?"

"Hold up." Dad motioned for the boys, and they helped him stand on his injured leg. With most of his weight distributed between them, he limped closer. "Are you saying Tamora fell from the skyscraper, too?"

I nodded. "Please—ask him."

Dad asked the general my question. The general grunted a harsh response.

"What'd he say?"

Dad looked at me. "He said Tamora likely died. Her body should be inside Emperor Qin's sarcophagus, lying beside him at this very moment."

I wanted proof Tamora was dead. The only way to know for certain was to venture back inside Emperor Qin's tomb, but in my family's current state—bruised and cut with possible broken bones—there was no way we could survive the trek. I would have to trust General Li's word that she didn't survive the fall.

Zac spoke up: "Wait, does that mean it's all over? We can go home now?"

Dad smiled. "Of course, son."

We glanced at General Li and the terracotta army. Thousands of terracotta warriors now stood behind the general in strict military ranks.

"But first," Dad added. "I think it's time we say goodbye."

Chapter 75

THE SUN WAS RISING AS we prepared to say goodbye. Its soft glow cast hues of ruddy orange across the sky, the east slowly turning from nighttime purple to daytime blue. The storm had dissipated. Faint stars could now be seen twinkling in the early morning light.

General Li stood before 6,000 terracotta warriors. The warriors looked just as they had inside their hangar back at the museum—in rows and columns forming military ranks.

The general bowed. "My friends," Dad translated his words, "we set out to defeat Emperor Qin, and with your combined bravery and strength, we avenged all of China."

The warriors hooted and hollered, and their cheers were infectious. I couldn't help but smile.

General Li raised a hand for quiet. The army settled down, and he resumed, "Yet our victory wouldn't have been possible if it weren't for the help of a young woman and the boldness of her family." He turned to face me. "You are a mighty warrior, Maddie Jones. Xièxiè."

"*Xièxiè!*" the army shouted all together, which Dad later told me meant *thanks*.

General Li bowed low. The army followed suit. I didn't know what to do with such an honor, so I mimicked the warriors and bowed in return. Dad and the boys joined me.

Afterward, the general mounted his war chariot and grasped the reins of his horses. The cavalry loomed behind him, horses pawing the ground and snorting, and their riders' clay jaws were set in determination. Beyond them, archers and infantrymen stood shoulder to shoulder ready to march out of town.

"What's gonna happen to you guys now?" I asked the general.

Dad interpreted my words, and General Li glanced back at his army. "The emperor's curse kept us from walking the halls of our ancestors for 2,000 years," he said. "Now . . . we rest. Our souls will finally know peace."

"Well," I said. "You deserve it."

He bowed again. And as I walked away from the Shaanxi Information Mansion with my dad and brothers, General Li transformed back into a clay statue. The terracotta warriors froze in place, and little fleeting lights drifted from their bodies as their souls ascended to heaven, free at last.

Chapter 76

TWENTY-FOUR HOURS LATER, after spending most of the day in a Chinese hospital to nurse our injuries, I got ready at the hotel in preparation for our flight home. The television was on. On almost every channel, news stations reported on the destruction in Xi'an, China. I ignored most of it as I brushed my teeth, mainly because it saddened me to hear that dozens of people throughout the city had lost their lives. Reporters blamed the destruction on a freak meteor shower.

I rinsed and spit, my bottom lip quivering. Although I'd already cried about it several times, the fact that people lost loved ones similar to how I had lost Mom hurt deeply.

The reporter on TV changed stories. Now she spoke about a mysterious event at the Shaanxi Information Mansion. I grabbed the TV remote and turned up the volume.

"*During the meteor shower last night,*" the reporter was saying. "*Somebody mysteriously transported thousands of terracotta warriors from their museum to the streets of Xi'an.*" Video footage taken from a helicopter showed an aerial shot of the terracotta army standing frozen as statues in front of the skyscraper.

A close-up zoomed in on the lead warrior in his war chariot. General Li's face was locked into an eternal stare, but a smirk touched his lips. I snickered because it was the closest thing to a smile I'd seen on the general's face. He seemed to be at peace for the first time in centuries.

"*Authorities are flabbergasted as to how this prank was achieved,*" the reporter continued. "*Even more mysterious is what happened at the Museum of Terracotta Warriors.*"

Video footage changed from the Shaanxi Information Mansion to the museum, where all of the warriors were missing from their hangar, horses and all. The footage transitioned to a shot of Emperor Qin's burial mound, where piles of dirt and debris loomed beside an opened set of ancient bronze doors. The silvery lightning streaks that marred the mound had faded away, so it looked as if the mound had been unearthed with heavy-duty machinery.

"*The Chinese government is furious. The Tomb of the First Qin Emperor appears to have been opened by none other than Ortega Industries' CEO, Rico Raja. Authorities found Mr. Raja's body inside the emperor's tomb, deceased, apparently killed by a booby-trap. They also discovered Emperor Qin's sarcophagus opened. His 2,000-year-old mummy rested inside, but it had been mutilated. An ancient Chinese sword was stabbed into his heart.*"

New footage showed the inside of Qin's burial chamber. Piles of jewels, coins, and precious stones glittered in green torchlight.

"*Riches beyond counting have been unearthed, but archaeologists around the world are up in arms that improper excavation techniques led to priceless artifacts being destroyed. Finally, one other body was discovered . . .*"

I held my breath. Here we go—news of Tamora Rose.

"*. . . at the tomb's entrance. It appears to be one of Mr. Raja's mercenaries who died of unknown causes. His body—along with Mr. Raja's—has been taken in for an autopsy.*"

"What?" I breathed. "No one else? What the fetch happened to Tamora?"

"We may never know," said my dad. I turned to see him leaning against the doorframe, arms folded across his chest.

"And you're okay with that?" I asked.

"Not really."

"What'd we do about it?"

"Nothing," he sighed. "Maybe Tamora lived. Maybe she died. If she survived, perhaps she'll have a change of heart and leave our family alone."

"What? Tamora's a witch. Her cold heart will never change."

Dad shrugged.

I contemplated telling Dad the truth about Mom's death. God knows I'd had several opportunities within the last twenty-four hours. But I hadn't been able to muster up the courage. You see, ten years ago when Mom passed away, Dad sank into a deep depression. He struggled with emotions and regrets and dark memories that would turn into nightmares. I can still remember hearing his sobs through the wall separating our bedrooms. I was only a child, but I remember. You don't easily forget stuff like that.

Thankfully, Dad came out of his depression . . . and I was willing to bet my brothers and I were the reason why. Now that I thought about it, Dad was better off not knowing how badly Tamora hurt our family.

At least for now.

"Everything all right, Maddie? You look deep in thought."

"Huh? Oh . . . yeah . . . I'm fine."

"All packed?"

"Pretty much," I said, shouldering my backpack. "When does the plane leave?"

"Couple hours. Don't forget Mom's necklace."

The compass necklace rested on the nightstand. I picked it up and put it on. Beside it was Rico's tape recorder. In the middle of the night, I'd awoken and couldn't go back to sleep, so I started listening to his tape. It was filled with Rico's words of encouragement, wisdom, memories, regrets, hopes, and dreams for his daughter. Most importantly, his words were filled with love. My eyes were still swollen from all the tears I'd shed listening to his message.

"Erm, Dad . . ."

"Yeah, Maddie?"

"Is it too late to change our flight to Boston?"

"Why? What's in Boston?"

I showed him Rico's tape recorder.

He smiled, though it lacked the warmth of happiness. "Sure thing, sweetie," he said. "I'll make a call."

Chapter 77

WE WAITED IN THE LOBBY of the Dana-Farber Children's Hospital in Boston. The lobby was warm and friendly, with hardwood floors and colorful décor appealing to younger children. Half the space was devoted to kids with a television playing cartoons, bean bag chairs, toys, puzzles, and coloring books. Two siblings were playing there now— a brother and sister around five and six years old. Neither of them looked sick, but I was reminded how they might be here to visit another sibling.

A middle-aged man in a suit and tie approached the reception desk. He signed in, then sat in a corner chair where he picked up a *Sports Illustrated* magazine to read while he waited.

I tried to picture Rico Raja doing the same, not as a powerful business tycoon of a weapons manufacturing company, but as a concerned parent who had come to visit his sick daughter. Seeing the man reading his magazine, and gazing at pictures on the walls of bald boys and girls smiling, made me realize why Rico did what he did.

Let me explain.

Parents of a kid with cancer will do whatever it takes to ensure the health of their child. This usually means extra hours at work to cover hospital expenses, long hours on the road traveling to treatment centers, comforting their child when treatments make them sick, and sacrificing dreams—all to save their child's life, or to make their child's remaining time as comfortable as possible. But for a guy like Rico, doing *whatever it takes* meant using the resources at his disposal.

Meaning, his mercenaries and guns.

He threw money at the problem, but that didn't heal Amira. He hired the finest doctors, but they couldn't eliminate her cancer. So Rico did what he thought was right—sought the fabled Elixir of Life from the Tomb of the First Qin Emperor of China.

What would I have done if I were in Rico's shoes? What would I have done to save my mom's life?

Anything, I thought. *I would sell my compass necklace or stop doing silly pranks. I'd do whatever it takes.*

I was beginning to finally understand Rico Raja. He wasn't the bad guy. He was simply a victim of a cruel world. Did that justify his actions? Hardly. But part of me wished things had turned out differently for him.

The receptionist slid back her glass partition window. "Amira is ready to see you now."

Dad stood and stretched. "Are you sure you want me to wait here?" he asked.

I nodded. "I think it's for the best. We have something in common with Amira that you don't."

"Which is . . . ?"

"We've both lost a parent."

"Oh," Dad cleared his throat. "Oh, yes, of course." He sat back down to wait, though I could see in his eyes something like sadness.

"Dad," I said. "We don't blame you for what happened to Mom."

He looked up and smiled. "I know that, sweetie."

"Just making sure. Are you gonna be okay for a bit?"

"Certainly," he said. "Take your time."

A nurse escorted us to Amira's room. My brothers and I followed her through a set of double doors and along a narrow corridor, which was lined with more framed pictures of smiling children. Doctors and nurses in white coats and scrubs walked in and out of doors as we passed. We entered an elevator and rode it up to the third floor, the nurse informing us that this level was the CANCER WARD. She led us past a door bearing the words RESEARCH AND DEVELOPMENT.

The ward was small and sterile with numerous windows creating a bright, cheery atmosphere. Yet every now and then, I heard distant coughing, reminding me how sick the kid-patients here truly were. The nurse stopped outside a room labeled 301. Underneath the number was a card in a brass holder. Handwritten on the card was the name, *Amira Raja.*

"Here we are," the nurse said, smiling. She motioned for us to go on inside.

I reached for the handle, but my hand was shaking as I reached for the doorknob. *Don't be nervous,* I told myself. *You made a promise. Let's keep it.* I swallowed, then opened the door and entered. Amira's hospital room was cozy and clean.

Flowers and get-well cards decorated the tables. Taped to white walls were colored drawings depicting a father and daughter. Morning sunlight streamed through the blinds.

Amira sat in her hospital bed with pillows propped behind her back. She was reading a book: *Harry Potter & the Goblet of Fire*—my favorite novel in the whole series. Amira looked close to my age, fourteen or fifteen. A framed photograph sat on her bedside table next to a glass of water and a thimble of colorful pills. I noticed the photo was of Amira and her dad. They were in the mountains somewhere, a snow-covered peak in the background, and the two of them were outfitted in hiking gear. Amira had the same dark complexion as Rico. In the photograph, her long black hair was beautiful and flowing. But right now, she was bald, which made her look even more like her father.

She glanced up as we entered. "You must be the visitors Stacey told me about."

"Erm, Stacey?" I asked.

"My nurse."

Stacey, the nurse who had escorted us here, stood at the door and smiled. "Are you going to behave yourself this time, Amira?"

Amira crossed her heart. "I'm a perfect angel."

"Mm-hmm." Stacey closed the door, giving us some quiet time with Amira.

Zac sat down in a chair near the window. "Doesn't sound like she trusts you," he said.

"Oh, Stacey's just angry at me. I tied a bunch of bedsheets together and attempted to escape."

Jason scoffed. "Why'd you do that?"

Amira lowered her voice to a whisper. "I heard a nasty rumor about my dad, but nobody will tell me what's going on. I must get out of here so I can find out if he's okay."

I squeezed Rico's tape recorder in my hand. I had hoped Amira already knew about the fate of her father. "So . . . are you enjoying *Goblet of Fire?*" I asked, sitting on the edge of her bed and changing subjects to avoid the painful conversation for just a bit longer.

Amira's face lit up. "Am I ever?! Harry, Hermione, and Ron just arrived at the Quidditch World Cup."

"Ooh, I loved that part."

For nearly an hour, Harry Potter dominated the conversation, and since both of my brothers had read the books, they chimed in every once in a while with comments about Malfoy or Dumbledore or You-Know-Who. Amira hadn't read all of the books, so we were careful not to spoil the story beyond what she'd already read. It was great to learn Amira and I both shared the same favorite character—Hermione—and loathed the same one as well—Professor Snape. It gave us common ground on which we could build a friendship.

"I tell you what," I said, grabbing a notepad from the table and scratching my phone number on it. "Let's make a promise. When you finish reading *Goblet of Fire*, we'll watch the movie together. We can Skype and eat popcorn. Will they let you do that here?"

Amira shrugged. "Maybe, and if not, I'll figure out a way." She winked at me.

I smiled. "Oh, I totally forgot to introduce myself. My name is Maddie Jones—and these two knuckleheads are my brothers, Jason and Zac." The boys waved sheepishly. "I think this is the beginning of a great friendship, Amira."

Amira looked puzzled. "Wait—are you guys part of a church or something? One that visits sick kids on the weekends?"

"No . . ." I said slowly.

"Then why'd you come to visit me?"

"Well, Amira, we erm . . ." I glanced at my brothers, fidgeting with the tape recorder in my hand. "We knew your father."

"You do?" she said, her smile widening. "Do you know what's happened to him? When did you see him last? Can you tell him to call me?"

I bit my lip. Tears formed at the corners of my eyes. Amira must've noticed.

"What is it?" she asked, looking from me to my brothers and back to me. "What's wrong with my papa?"

I inhaled a deep breath, then I told her the story of what had happened over the past several days. I didn't leave anything out (well, that's not true. I kept hidden the fact that Rico kidnapped my dad, instead deciding to tell Amira our fathers worked cooperatively together to find the Elixir of Life). When I finished, Amira was crying, and I set the tape recorder on her lap.

"Your father loved you very much," I said. "He went to great lengths to find you a cure. He wanted you to have this."

Amira dried her eyes on her bedsheet. "Sorry for crying," she said.

"Don't be," I said. "When my mom passed away, I cried all the time. Crying is good. It helps to get the emotions out.

So cry as much as you need. And when you're ready, you can check out your papa's gift. I wish my mom had given me something like that."

Amira picked up the tape recorder with trembling hands. "What is it?"

"It's your papa's voice," I said. "He recorded a message for you." I stood, and gave my brothers a look signaling this was our cue to leave. They nodded, and slowly made their way to the door. "Just press play and—"

She pressed play, and static sounded before steadily coming into focus.

"I'll be in touch," I whispered, but I don't think she heard me. Amira's attention was solely on the voice now speaking through the tape recorder's tiny speaker.

"Amira . . . my darling . . . if you're hearing this . . . then I have failed to find a cure for your cancer . . . and it means . . . in all likelihood . . . that I am dead."

Amira sobbed.

I eased to the door, Rico's last words fading away as I closed it gently behind me.

Chapter 78

A FEW DAYS AFTER VISITING Amira, I sat on a bench outside the Evansville History Museum enjoying some peace and quiet for a change. Noonday traffic flooded the street while the sounds of city life filled my ears: horns honking, indistinct chatter from pedestrians walking the sidewalk, and pigeons cooing. I closed my eyes to listen, relaxed and content, looking forward to having dinner with my dad when he got off work at five o'clock. After all the scary stuff we'd been through, it felt really nice knowing our family was safe.

"I figured I might find you here," said a stern, female voice.

I opened my eyes to find Detective Murphy looming over me. Her ponytail was pulled back tightly, and she donned civilian clothes instead of her badge—blue jeans and a white Tee beneath a black leather jacket. Her arm was in a sling. I could see cuts on her face and a purple bruise crawling up her neck.

"Detective Murphy," I said. "When did you get out of the hospital?"

"They released me this morning," she said, sitting down beside me. "I never got a chance to thank you for saving my life."

"I didn't, either," I said. There was an awkward pause, then we both said, "Thanks," at the same time.

She smiled. "I stopped by the Station this morning. Officer Trent—the cop with the freckles you met when we investigated your house—filled me in on everything that happened after the car crash."

"Did he now?"

"He says you escaped the hospital—then burglarized your dad's museum. Breaking and entering is a serious offense, Miss Jones." She paused to look at me, but I didn't say a word. "But the charges were dropped. How on earth did you manage that?"

"Well, I do have an in with the museum curator," I said. "He's kind of my dad."

"Saved his life, too—from what I've heard."

I shrugged.

"What I still can't figure out is how you kids traveled to China."

A memory of mummies and a dark crate made me shudder. I hoped we never had to travel as mummies ever again. "Mum's the word," I finally said.

"Mum, huh? Why do I get the feeling you've broken about a hundred laws?"

I smirked.

She reached into her jacket with her good hand and pulled out her cell phone. She powered it on and opened the YouTube app. "There's a video I wanted to show you," she said, handing me the phone. "It's gone viral in only a matter of days."

I glanced at the phone's screen. The video was titled *Old Chinese Magic or Government Cover-up*. It had over ten million views even though it was only a few days old. Curious, I hit play.

The footage was shaky and a bit blurry, but I recognized the scene at once. It was recorded in the streets of Xi'an, China outside the apartment building we marched by with General Li and the terracotta army. I stood beside General Li in his war chariot as it rumbled down the road, wearing bronze armor and holding a spear. Behind me came the cavalry of bronze horses with Zac waving at bystanders, saying, "Nothing to see here. Move along." Behind the cavalry, row after row of terracotta warriors marched past.

The video ended with a black screen and white text: WHAT THE MEDIA ISN'T SHOWING US. THE TERRACOTTA WARRIORS WERE ALIVE. WHO ARE THE AMERICANS? WE MAY NEVER KNOW.

"Do you know anything about it?" asked Detective Murphy.

"No," I said, handing back her phone. "You can't believe everything you see on the internet."

"Mm-hmm." Detective Murphy slipped her phone back into her jacket pocket. "There's one last thing." She revealed a manila envelope. "I had a look at your record."

"Oh, yeah?"

"There are some silly crimes in here," she said, rifling through its pages. "And I think I've finally got you figured out. All of your crimes are pranks. There's nothing criminal about them. You're simply a prankster, Miss Jones—not a juvenile—and I think you like people believing you're harder than you really are."

I feigned shock. "Detective—such an accusation."

"Don't worry," she said, standing. "I'll let you maintain your image. But you should know—I've got my eye on you."

"And I wouldn't have it any other way," I said. "My pranks will taste that much sweeter knowing I did them right under your nose."

Detective Murphy shook her head, but she was smiling. "You're a real piece of work, girl."

Chapter 79

THE ROCK WALL IN GYM class used to intimidate me. But not today. I scaled its wall faster than I ever had before, hoisting myself up one colorful handhold at a time. Heck, sometimes I skipped handholds and bounded right past them. What did I have to fear? I was tethered with a safety harness. And this obstacle was nothing compared to scaling a 2,000-year-old tomb or hanging on for dear life from a fifty-story skyscraper.

"Slow down, Jones, or you're gonna make a mistake and fall," shouted Coach Sinclair, my pudgy P.E. instructor with pit stains beneath his arms.

I ignored him and climbed even quicker. I reached the top, slapped a bell, and kicked off the wall to repel down as it chimed. I hit the ground in a crouch, one hand touching the basketball court. Coach Sinclair stood over me with a stopwatch in hand.

"Impressive, Jones—that's a new record."

"Really?" I said, standing and unbuckling my harness. "I beat my old time?"

"No—it's a new record for the school. Geez Louise, girl, what's gotten into you?"

"Ah, it was easy," I said. "All I had to do was pretend giant scorpions were trying to kill me."

Coach Sinclair furrowed his brow. "Er—what?"

I smiled, not bothering to explain, and stepped out of my harness. I went to grab a sweat towel, but Coach Sinclair stopped me.

"I'm serious, Jones. Last week you couldn't reach the top. How'd you improve so quickly?"

"You wouldn't believe me if I told you, Coach."

"Try me."

"Okay," I said, taking a deep breath. "My dad was kidnapped by the CEO of a weapons manufacturing company. My brothers and I flew to China to save him, witnessed a 2,000-year-old mummy come to life, escaped a deadly tomb maze, and then I helped lead an ancient army into battle. During the process, I was forced to overcome my fear of climbing by scaling a tomb's walls while being chased by giant killer scorpions."

Coach Sinclair scoffed. "You expect me to believe all of that?"

"No," I said. "But you asked."

He shook his head, then shooed me away with his clipboard. "All right, Jones, get out of my sight."

I turned and darted for the locker room, grinning broadly. I had conquered the rock wall. I felt like I could conquer anything. If any more bad guys come sniffing around, they'd better think twice before messing with Maddie Jones.

Epilogue

SHE WOKE IN UTTER DARKNESS.

The first thing she noticed was the smell. An overly sweet stench of her perfume mixed with the ripeness of a decaying corpse. Something brushed against her cheek. She reached to feel what it was, and her fingers found the unmistakable outline of a human skull with hollowed-out eye sockets.

She sat bolt upright, looking around. Everything was shadowed in darkness.

"No," she gasped, fear churning in the pit of her stomach. A hunch told her she knew what room she had awoken, but she must be certain. She reached into her pocket and pulled out a cigarette lighter. Two strikes and the tiny flame illuminated her immediate surroundings.

A golden sarcophagus inlaid with emeralds, jades, and rubies.

Mounds of gemstones and coins.

And a rotting corpse in a tattered yellow robe, which she was now lying beside.

She screamed and leapt out of the coffin. The lighter's flame went out. Her shout echoed off the tomb's walls. Another noise joined in—shrieks of giant scorpions and the clacking of their pincers.

"No," she cried. The creatures had heard her.

Desperate for light, she struck the lighter, but it wouldn't ignite. She tried again, but a flame wouldn't spark. The scorpions' shrieks grew louder. They were coming closer.

"Light, damn it—light—"

A tiny flame ignited. She held the lighter high. Giant scorpions flooded into the chamber through cracks in the walls, ceiling, and floor. They swarmed the tomb and circled the sarcophagus like a sea of dark water, ready to drown her in a wave of painful death.

"Stay back!" she shouted, but it was the small illumination the scorpions steered away from. Her eyes raked over her surroundings. Just on the cusp of firelight, an open door loomed with a stairwell leading up.

If I can get to that door . . .

She cupped her hand to protect the lighter's flame, and eased toward the stairwell. Scorpions skittered to stay in the darkness. A quivering smile touched her lips. All she had to do was keep the light ablaze and she'd be able to escape.

Her foot struck something hard. She stumbled and the fire snuffed out.

Scorpions shrieked. Claws scraped across stone. She fumbled with the lighter. A flame ignited on the third attempt. The creatures hissed at the sudden illumination and retreated, but only a little. She blew out a breath.

Just a little farther . . .

Just a little farther and she would be gone from this accursed tomb. Free from these deadly scorpions. Then the real challenge would begin. Enacting vengeance against the Jones family for the death of her son.

"Scorpions first, love," Tamora told herself. "Revenge later."

The End

Continue reading Maddie's story in Grave of Robin Hood: A Maddie Jones Mystery, Book 2!

Don't miss updates on new releases from Mark Douglas, Jr. Sign up for his mailing list at www.Mark–DouglasJr.com and receive a FREE Maddie Jones mystery!

If you enjoyed reading this book, I would sincerely appreciate it if you would give me a review! It only takes a few words, but it means so much. Thank you!

Join Mark's Newsletter

Want to be notified the minute Mark's next book is released? Sign up for his newsletter at www.Mark–DouglasJr.com to get cover reveals, exclusive content, and new release announcements. Plus, you'll receive a FREE Maddie Jones mystery for signing up!

About the Author

MARK DOUGLAS, JR. finds inspiration from history and cranks it up to eleven. After graduating college, Mark went on to teach history to teenagers. Each day, the kids participated in a program called Drop Everything and Read. However, many of Mark's students hated reading, so he began reading aloud to them. Mark read Wednesday Wars, Treasure Island, and the Egypt Game. But the kids enjoyed Percy Jackson & the Olympians most. Several kids checked out the series from the library so they could read ahead.

Inspired, Mark embarked on his own storytelling journey. And a decade later, he's telling stories about the exploits of spunky teenage heroine Maddie Jones.

Want More?

Love Mark's books? Join his mailing list at <u>www.Mark–DouglasJr.com</u> to be notified of new releases and giveaways!

You can also hang out with him on Facebook, Instagram, Twitter, and Goodreads.

Want even more? Subscribe to Mark's YouTube channel or join him on TikTok to get insider information on his writing process, how he finds inspiration for his stories, and what it's like to be an author. He also creates fun games and challenges for his viewers.

Connect With Mark Online:
<u>www.Mark–DouglasJr.com</u>